A Deadly Seri
Co1

CW00523950

Heavenly Highland Inn Cozy
Mystery Series

Cindy Bell

Copyright © 2014 Cindy Bell

All rights reserved.

ISBN-13: 978-1503216396

ISBN-10: 150321639X

More Cozy Mysteries by Cindy Bell

Dune House Cozy Mystery Series

Seaside Secrets

Boats and Bad Guys

Treasured History

Hidden Hideaways

Heavenly Highland Inn Cozy Mystery Series

Murdering the Roses

Dead in the Daisies

Killing the Carnations

Drowning the Daffodils

Suffocating the Sunflowers

Books, Bullets and Blooms

A Deadly serious Gardening Contest

Table of Contents

Chapter One

Vicky was very excited. The beautiful gardens surrounding the Heavenly Highland Inn had caught the attention of one of the trendiest gardening magazines in the US. 'Garnish your Garden' was a magazine that was packed from cover to cover with unique and modern ways to turn your garden into the centerpiece of your home. When one of the editors stayed in Highland at the Heavenly Highland Inn, he was so impressed with what he saw that he insisted their next contest be hosted there.

When Sarah got the call with the request she was elated. Everyone at the inn was, because they knew that it would not only bring some new guests from all over the country, but it would be a lot of fun to host the contest. They had booked two weeks in advance so Sarah, Vicky, and Aunt Ida had been working non-stop in the gardens to make sure that there was enough room for the contest, and of course a beautiful display to be seen.

Sarah was in charge of the accommodation and the catering. Vicky was in charge of setting up booths in the banquet hall for the vendors as well as coordinating the decorations in the gardens and ensuring that everyone who visited would have a breathtaking experience. With her fiancé, Mitchell's, help she had erected several wooden stands for displays and for the guests to shelter in. It had been a true test of their recent engagement, especially when Vicky had accidentally hit Mitchell's thumb with a hammer. The memory of that event was still fresh in Vicky's mind as she stood in the gardens the morning before the contest. She was there to do a final check that everything was in place, from seating to lighting, to the flooring for the musicians that would be playing throughout the two days of the contest.

But really she knew that everything was already perfect, she was enjoying the morning sunshine and the anticipation of the gardens being filled with happy guests the next day.

"Good morning, my blossom," Mitchell called out from the path that wound around the side of the inn, beyond the pool and the employees' quarters, to the gardens. Vicky grinned at the way his southern drawl turned anything he said into something she wanted to remember forever.

"Morning," she called out as she met him at the end of the path. Since he had been promoted to detective he no longer had to wear a uniform. Vicky missed it just a little bit. He drew her in for a deep kiss, sending butterflies dancing in her stomach. When he released her she cringed at the sight of his bandaged thumb.

"Does it still hurt?" she asked as she looked into his eyes.

He pursed his lips briefly and cast his piercing

blue eyes over hers.

"Let's just say I'm not going to trust you with a hammer any time soon," he chuckled.

"It was an accident," she grimaced and hugged him gently. "I'm so sorry."

"Nothing to apologize for," he said calmly and brushed a hand through her dark brown hair. "It's quite obvious that my thumb did something to offend you."

"Ha ha," Vicky said with a slow smile, her deep green eyes dancing. "I'm serious, how is it feeling?"

"It's fine," he promised. "So, is everything ready?" he asked as he glanced over the gardens. "It couldn't be more beautiful," he smiled with approval.

"I think we're all set," Vicky replied proudly. "The gardens were gorgeous before, but now I think they are fit for a magazine. Those areas over there are for the gardens that people will set up for the contest."

"I still don't see how anyone can create such incredible gardens in such a short period of time," he said and shook his head with amazement.

"Well, that's why it's a contest," she grinned. "The stands turned out wonderfully."

"Yes, they did," he said proudly. "We really do make a great team."

"Except for the injuries," Vicky reminded him with a grimace.

"Even with injuries," he smiled and kissed her cheek. "But seriously, no more hammers."

"No more hammers," she promised with a guilty smile.

"I only have a little time before I have to head to work," Mitchell explained. "I think Sheriff McDonnell thinks he needs to work me twice the amount of hours in order to make up for my promotion."

"I think he just knows what a great detective you are," Vicky replied proudly.

"Ever since the engagement he has been bugging me to let him know when I need to take time off for the wedding," Mitchell mentioned casually. Vicky tensed at the question. She covered it with a smile.

"Well, he'll be the third one to know, right?" she grinned.

"I hope I'm in those first two," Mitchell said with a short laugh. "Or, are you and Sarah planning things behind my back?"

Vicky shook her head and smiled. Her sister, Sarah, was not only her sister, but her best friend. Vicky secretly knew that Sarah probably would be the second to know.

"Well, there is the wedding season to think about, and with this contest..." she began to make excuses.

"Sweetheart," Mitchell cupped her cheeks

gently with his hands and looked deeply into her eyes. "I'm not trying to rush anything. I want you to marry me, when you are ready, and not a moment sooner."

"I am ready," Vicky insisted, a little worried that he would think that she wasn't.

"Oh good, because I called the Justice of the Peace," Mitchell began in a serious tone.

"Mitchell," Vicky gasped and laughed when he winked. He kissed her softly and then looked into her eyes again.

"I mean it, Vicky. This is a big step. I know that you love me, and I am willing to wait. I'd rather know that you were absolutely certain, than think that you might have set a date just to please me," he raised an eyebrow slightly. "Don't worry I'll have you barefoot and pregnant in no time."

"What?" Vicky glared at him.

"Don't hurt me!" Mitchell grimaced. "Are

there any hammers around?"

"You are so silly," Vicky shook her head and then kissed him. "Maybe you can have me barefoot on the beach on our honeymoon, but that's all I'm promising."

"I'll take it," Mitchell grinned then glanced at his watch. "Sorry, I have to get going, call me if you need anything. Okay?"

"I will," Vicky promised. "Love you," she added. Mitchell smiled as if hearing those words still lit a fire in his heart.

"Love you, too," he murmured and kissed her once more before walking off.

***

After Mitchell left, Vicky stepped inside the inn. Sarah was already behind the front desk going over last minute details.

"Morning, Sis," Vicky said as she walked up to her. "Are you excited?"

"Very," Sarah replied in a tight voice. Vicky narrowed her eyes slightly. Sarah's blonde hair looked a little frazzled, and her brown eyes were tense and focused on the computer in front of her.

"Is something wrong?" Vicky frowned as she studied her sister. "You don't seem very excited."

"I'm sorry," Sarah shook her head as she looked up at her. "I just want everything to be perfect, but something is telling me that everything is going to go wrong."

"I'm sure everything will be fine. Do you need help with anything?" Vicky asked quickly. "I'm done in the gardens, I can help you with whatever you need."

"Thanks, Vicky," Sarah sighed with relief. "Everything is ready, it's just that sometimes I get a little wound up."

Vicky smiled sympathetically. She knew that

Sarah had the inn to run, plus a family at home that she had to be present for.

"Have you been getting any rest?" she asked with concern. "Do you want me to take the boys for a bit?"

"No, it's okay," Sarah insisted. "Phil has been helping me so much. He knows how important this contest is to me and he has even offered to watch the boys all weekend so I can stay here and make sure everything goes smoothly."

"That's good," Vicky smiled with approval. Since Sarah and Vicky's parents had died in a car accident, Vicky knew that Sarah had been shouldering the burden of responsibility a lot longer than she had. Phil had been an amazing help as the sisters went through their grieving process together. Vicky was relieved that her sister had married such a wonderful man. "But remember this is supposed to be fun, too," Vicky said. "Don't make me stick Aunt Ida on you."

"Oh no, please don't," Sarah laughed. "I promise that I will have fun."

Sarah and Vicky had grown up in the Heavenly Highland Inn, which their parents had run until their death. Aunt Ida had been a presence in their lives before that, a fun and slightly crazy aunt that always had the strangest gifts and advice to give. After their parents died, she had become more of a motherly figure to Sarah and Vicky, though she still had plenty of her quirky moments and insisted on fun at all times.

"Good," Vicky said, feeling a little better as she studied Sarah's smile. "I think everything is going to go perfectly. I can't wait to meet the contestants."

"Me neither," Sarah agreed. "From what I've read about them, they each have very different ideas and talents. It looks like we'll have three for the contest tomorrow."

"Only three?" Vicky asked with surprise. "I

had planned for four."

"I only have three registered," Sarah shrugged. "Maybe one couldn't attend."

"Either way it will be great," Vicky promised.

"I hope so," Sarah said nervously. "I think Chef Henry is ready to throw me in the pool."

"Oh no, you haven't been checking in on him have you?" Vicky asked with a grimace. Henry was very passionate about his work and liked to be left alone in the kitchen.

"I wouldn't say checking," Sarah hummed softly under her breath, a sure sign that she was fibbing.

"Okay, what would you call it?" Vicky laughed.

"I would say it was a friendly visit to the kitchen," Sarah stated flatly.

"But Chef Henry didn't see it that way?" Vicky assumed.

"Let's just say, he knows how to use a spatula as a weapon," Sarah giggled.

"Note to self, no hammers or spatulas laying around," Vicky laughed.

"Speaking of hammers," Sarah said smoothly. "Was that Mitchell I saw walking towards the gardens?"

"It was," Vicky replied with a faint blush. "He's been finding a way to give me a good morning kiss each day."

"Ah, love," Sarah sighed dreamily. "Do you know that Phil still waits for me to get home before he will go to bed? Even if I'm super later?"

"That's so sweet," Vicky smiled.

"He is sweet," Sarah agreed with a faraway look in her eyes. "I'm not sure how we both got so lucky."

"Must have something to do with Aunt Ida," Vicky said with a nod of confidence. "I bet she cast some kind of spell to make sure we'd meet the men of our dreams."

"I wouldn't put it past her," Sarah laughed. "Have you talked to Linda about the rooms?" she asked, her mind immediately turning back to work. Sarah was much more organized than Vicky could ever dream of being. She had no problem running the inn. Vicky on the other hand had more of a creative mind, which was why it was her job to host and decorate events like weddings and parties that were held at the inn.

"Me neither," Vicky agreed. "She has that witchy way about her, you know."

"You two must be talking about me," a boisterous voice called out from the front entrance of the inn. Standing in the doorway was their aunt, although it was a little hard to recognize her in the outfit she was wearing. The neon yellow spandex was enough to make Vicky's eyes burn.

"Aunt Ida, your ears must have been burning," Sarah smiled and tried not to laugh at the outfit.

"What in the world are you up to, now?" Vicky giggled as she walked towards her aunt to take a closer look at her outfit.

"Rex and I have decided that we're going to sign up for a marathon," Ida said proudly.

"Well, we're talking about it," Rex stammered out as he stepped in behind Ida. He was also wearing skin tight spandex, though his outfit was a deep blue with a few neon stripes.

Vicky raised an eyebrow and smiled.

"That is quite an adventure to take," she said.

"It's just what we need to remind us of how capable we are," Ida said with confidence. "We need to get in shape, so that we can live our lives to the fullest."

Vicky glanced past Ida to Rex. She wondered

if he was as keen on the idea.

"I think it's great," Vicky said. "Just don't overdo it, Aunt Ida."

"You see," Ida said, getting irate. "When you say things like that it just proves that this marathon must be done. When I cross that finish line, you won't be telling me not to overdo it."

"I'm sure Vicky didn't mean anything by it," Rex said calmly. He had a very mild attitude compared to what Vicky expected a biker to be like.

"I didn't," Vicky agreed. "There's no doubt in my mind that you can do anything that you put your mind to, Aunt Ida."

"Good," Ida nodded. "Because we're not only going to run that marathon, we're going to win it!"

Rex rolled his eyes and groaned. "There's no way I'm winning a marathon, Ida."

"You say that now," Ida said stubbornly. "But

that's only because we haven't started training. Just wait and you'll see how strong you are."

"If these clothes don't kill me first," he said with a chuckle.

"You'll survive," Aunt Ida insisted and gave him a light swat in the gut.

Sarah, who had been trying valiantly not to laugh, burst into laughter at the sound of Ida's slap against Rex's spandex covered stomach.

"Very funny," Ida huffed. "I'll have you know that there is no reason I can't be as fit, if not fitter than you both."

"I'm not winning any marathons," Vicky admitted and giggled. Sarah cleared her throat and tried to keep a straight face.

"I think it's a wonderful idea, Aunt Ida," she said with a smile.

"I'm glad you do," Ida said. "Now, if you don't mind, Rex and I have to get back to our training."

"But we just walked a mile," Rex said.

"Now, we're going to run it!" Ida said enthusiastically.

Rex looked at Sarah and Vicky for help but they were too busy trying not to laugh at the look of Aunt Ida retreating through the door. Rex hung his head and then followed after her.

"They seem to be getting pretty serious," Sarah commented when they were gone.

"Has Aunt Ida ever been serious about anyone?" Vicky laughed and shook her head.

"I might have said the same about you, Vicky," Sarah reminded her. "Love shows up when it's ready."

"Speaking of," Vicky grinned as she glanced at the entrance of the inn. "Did you miss me already?" she asked as Mitchell walked back in, with a tall, thin man following after him.

"I found one of your contestants," Mitchell

explained with a warm smile. "He was looking for directions at the gas station, so I decided to give him an escort. That couldn't be construed as an excuse to see you again this morning, could it?"

"I think it could," Vicky replied with a wink.

"Welcome," Sarah said with a smile to the man standing nervously behind Mitchell.

"I know I'm early," he said with a frown. "I just like to get the lay of the land."

"I understand that," Sarah replied. "I'll just get you checked in. Your name?"

"Baron," he replied.

"Is that first or last?" Sarah asked.

"It's just Baron," he replied.

"Okay," Sarah replied with a smile and walked over to the computer to log him into the system. Baron followed after her, leaving Mitchell and Vicky alone for a few moments.

"So, tell me more about the contest," Mitchell

pleaded with interest. "That way I can know when the best time is to drop in for a visit."

"There's going to be a big ceremony first thing in the morning tomorrow," Vicky explained. "That way they can introduce the contestants and talk about the schedule of the events."

"I think that I'd like to be there for that," Mitchell grinned. "Are you going to be presenting I hope?"

"I hope not," Vicky laughed. "It will be up to Ray Baxter, he's the one running the contest."

"I just know that you're going to end up on a magazine cover," Sarah said with a soft giggle as she walked back over. Baron had already headed up to his room with one of the staff members toting his bags. "No matter what you do don't let Aunt Ida dress you."

"Nope, jeans only," Vicky said sternly, though she had to chuckle a little at what she imagined Ida could come up with. "I might just be getting my hands dirty."

"Are you going to be doing some gardening?" Mitchell asked with interest.

"All I know for sure is that I'm going to make sure that I have a chance to learn some things from these contestants," Vicky explained. "In order to qualify they had to show proof of creating some beautiful gardens and most were very experienced contestants. It never hurts to get some tips from the pros," she added.

"Sounds like a wonderful day," Mitchell said. "I'll do what I can to be here for most of it."

"I know you will, hon," Vicky said and gave him a light peck on his cheek. "But your work is important, if you can't make it, I understand."

"Aw," Sarah purred and winked lightly at the two of them.

Vicky shot her a look of annoyance.

"Speaking of weddings," Sarah began in a

lighthearted voice.

"No one was speaking of weddings," Vicky pointed out sternly.

"But we are now," Mitchell smiled slowly and looked into Vicky's eyes.

"I'm not," Vicky said, her frustration growing. "I've got to go check on the catering," she added and slipped away from Mitchell. She could feel him watching her as she walked away.

"Don't take it personally," Sarah said in a hushed tone to Mitchell. "She'll talk about it soon enough," she winked at Mitchell.

Mitchell managed a smile, but it didn't quite reach his eyes.

***

Vicky retreated to the relative safety of Chef Henry's kitchen.

"Not again," he groaned when he heard her walk in.

"Don't worry, I'm not really checking on the food," Vicky said. "I'm hiding out."

"Not from your fiancé I hope?" Chef Henry asked as he tilted his head towards the large bay window that overlooked the gardens. Mitchell had taken the back way to get around to the front of the inn.

"Maybe," she murmured guiltily.

"What did you do now?" he asked as he added a few garnishes to the lunch plates he was preparing.

"I didn't do anything wrong," Vicky said defensively. "I did say yes to the proposal, remember?"

"Saying yes, and doing yes, are two different things," Henry chuckled and shook his head.

"Lots of people have long engagements,"

Vicky pointed out as she shifted uneasily into a chair.

"Sure they do, if they're in college, or they're waiting for a big promotion," Henry agreed mildly. "Which of those applies to you?" he raised an eyebrow.

Vicky rolled her eyes and sighed. She had come into the kitchen to avoid the questions that she was now facing yet again. She decided to turn the tables on Henry.

"So, how are the food preparations going?" Vicky asked in a professional tone.

"Out!" Chef Henry demanded, waving the large spatula he had just picked up at her. "Out of here, now!"

Vicky laughed as she dodged a swat and ducked out of the kitchen.

After leaving the kitchen, Vicky stepped back into the main lobby of the inn. There was soft music playing. A lot of the flowers from the garden had been bundled and placed around the lobby to spruce it up. The vendors' booths were set up in the banquet hall, with vendors already setting up. She found Sarah sorting through some paperwork.

"Sorry about earlier," Sarah said the moment Vicky paused in front of the desk.

"It's okay," Vicky said casually. Sarah looked up guiltily and met her younger sister's eyes. She was silent for a long moment, and then as if she could not hold it any longer, she spoke again.

"But really, what's going on with the wedding date? You're going to have it here, aren't you?" she pressed.

"Sarah," Vicky growled with exasperation. "I've only been engaged for a little while, can't I just enjoy that?"

"Of course you can," Sarah said thoughtfully. "I just wonder how Mitchell is feeling about that."

"I'm sure he's fine," Vicky replied. "He told me

he wants me to be ready."

"Are you?" Sarah asked as she looked directly at Vicky.

"How am I supposed to know?" Vicky bit back. "It's not like there's some big sign that shows up in front of my eyes and tells me I'm ready."

Sarah tilted her head back and forth as she considered that.

"Oh, look at the time, the other guests should be arriving," Vicky said smoothly. "I'll wait in the front for them."

"Mmhm," Sarah nodded, knowing her sister was only trying to avoid her questions.

Chapter Two

As the rest of the contestants began to arrive, Vicky stood at the entrance of the Heavenly Highland Inn. She was relieved that the inn featured a very large driveway as it was already full of vendor vans and more vans were piling into the spaces available. One contestant even hired a small moving truck. Vicky was beginning to feel less confident that they had allowed adequate space for the gardens that these contestants were intending to create.

Vicky took a deep breath and smiled as a couple walked towards her. The woman had long, shiny blonde hair, so shiny that Vicky had to do a double take. Was it possible that the woman actually had glitter in her hair? The man with his arm looped through hers was very tall, with a slender frame and a slight mustache. They made a lovely couple.

"Hello and welcome to the Heavenly Highland Inn," Vicky said warmly when they reached the entrance.

"Please tell me this place is bigger than it looks from the outside," the woman said anxiously.

"Our property goes back several acres," Vicky explained.

"We're the Thomsons," the man explained. "I'm Vaughn and this is my wife Lauren," he smiled at her and patted her hand. "She takes her gardening deadly seriously."

"It is a contest," Lauren pointed out in a snippy tone. "It's more than my gardening, it's my career."

Vaughn nodded. "Of course it is, dear," he replied.

"If you'd like I can give you a tour of the gardens as soon as all of the contestants have arrived," Vicky offered. "Until then, can I show you to your room?"

"I would rather see the gardens first," Lauren said impatiently.

"I'm sorry but the host of the contest has very strict rules. All of the contestants must be introduced to the gardens at the same time. Though it looks like everyone is arriving, so you shouldn't have to wait very long," she added.

"If you say so," Lauren sighed. "I suppose going to our rooms would be best then."

"Right this way," Vicky said and nodded to Sarah who was stepping out to greet the other guests. "Sarah, this is Vaughn and Lauren Thomson. This is my sister Sarah," Vicky explained. "We run the inn together."

"It's a pleasure to meet you both," Sarah smiled. "Please don't hesitate to let us know if you need anything during your stay here."

"Thank you," Vaughn said graciously. Lauren was busy scoping out the other contestants that were approaching the inn.

"Can you believe they let Margaret Reye in the contest?" she said scornfully. She was glaring at a willowy woman who was struggling with a satchel of spades and handheld rakes as she stepped in the door.

"Lauren, you promised," Vaughn warned her.

"I know, I know, I have to be nice," Lauren rolled her eyes.

"I'll take you to your room," Vicky offered in an attempt to diffuse the tension that was building. She had the feeling that it would be best to try to keep the contestants separated as much as possible. The couple followed after Vicky as she led them to the elevator. They had given the contestants rooms on the top floor so that they would all have a view of the gardens. They were also the largest rooms at the inn. With money being no object for the magazine, they had asked for the best accommodation.

"How quaint," Lauren said as she looked over the homey decor. Vicky was nearly offended by her comment, until Lauren continued. "This is very refreshing compared to those cookie cutter hotels we usually have to stay in for these contests. It's almost like I feel at home," she added with a short laugh. Vicky had to smile at her words. It was exactly the feeling that she and Sarah strived to create for their guests.

"Again, if there's anything either of you need, feel free to call down to the front desk," Vicky said.

"What's this?" Lauren asked as she stared at the glasses of champagne that were waiting for them in their room.

"Oh, complimentary champagne for all of the contestants," Vicky replied proudly. It was a touch she had added herself, to give the room a celebratory feel.

"I don't drink," Lauren said flatly. She picked up the champagne glasses and walked towards the bathroom to toss the champagne down the sink.

"I do," Vaughn said swiftly and snatched one of the glasses from Lauren's hand.

"You shouldn't," Lauren countered and continued to the bathroom to toss out the champagne. Vicky frowned as Lauren handed her the glass. "Please, do not deliver any more alcohol to this room."

"I'll make a note of that on your account," Vicky replied. "I'm sorry for the confusion."

"Don't make a note of it," Vaughn snapped. "I like to have a drink now and then, and there is nothing wrong with that."

Lauren glared at him. "You know that I prefer to have an alcohol free environment, Vaughn."

"And yet, you insisted I come along," Vaughn said with a strained smile. Vicky was silent through their spat. She felt incredibly uncomfortable witnessing it, but it was nothing she hadn't seen before. Travel could really test a couple's relationship.

"Whatever you two decide we will certainly accommodate," Vicky said with a broad smile. "I'll leave you two to get settled in."

Lauren didn't even bother to look at her as she stormed back into the bathroom and closed the door. Vaughn shrugged and finished his champagne. He handed the glass back to Vicky.

"Thanks, it was delicious," he said.

"You're quite welcome," Vicky said and slipped out the door as quickly as she could. She rode down in the elevator, hanging onto the glasses. The entire encounter had been awkward. She dropped the glasses off in the restaurant and then headed back into the main lobby.

Sarah was waiting for her with wide eyes. She was obviously anxious to tell Vicky about something.

"Do you know who that was?" she asked.

"Lauren and Vaughn Thomson," Vicky replied with a furrowed brow.

"Yes, of course that's their names," Sarah said with a frown. "But do you know who they are?"

"Apparently you know more than I do," Vicky frowned back. "So spit it out!"

Sarah glanced over her shoulder to make sure that no one was close enough to hear her. Then she spoke in a hushed voice, "Vaughn Thomson is running for District Attorney, and he's very likely to be elected."

"Wow," Vicky said, equally impressed. She was always excited when a celebrity stayed at the inn. "I guess we better make sure we take good care of him."

"Absolutely," Sarah agreed as she smiled at some new guests who were entering. "Let's just hope everything goes smoothly this weekend," she added quickly before heading off to greet the guests.

Vicky stepped behind the desk and perused the list of guests that had not yet arrived. It was going to be a very busy weekend. Sarah's words hung ominously in her mind. She hoped that everything would go smoothly, too, but with so much attention on the inn she was sure there would be a few snafus. She had gone over everything with the staff and everyone seemed to be on the same page, but all it took was one slip up for everything to change. She could only hope that slip up would be minor enough to be fixed quickly.

"Excuse me," a nasally voice said from behind the computer monitor.

"Yes, how may I help you?" Vicky asked with a warm smile. The woman before her was short and round at the waist. She had auburn hair that was cut at sharp angles and no longer than her earlobe. Her blouse was covered with big flowers of all different colors.

"My name is Roxanne Duran," she replied with a tight smile. "I'm one of the contestants in the contest."

"Oh?" Vicky replied. The name wasn't familiar to her and she had made sure that she knew the names of all of the contestants. She began tapping on the keyboard. "I'm sorry I don't have your name here," Vicky frowned.

"Not this again," Roxanne sighed. "I don't know how this always happens to me. I am a contestant," she said firmly. "I have the paperwork right here," she slid some papers across the counter to Vicky. Vicky looked over the papers and nodded.

"I'm so sorry for the inconvenience, we must have received an incomplete list," she said, mystified as she had confirmed the list twice.

"Oh, I'm sure you didn't," Roxanne huffed. "This happens all of the time. You see the men and women in this contest do not play fair. If it's not one thing then it's another. Once my flight was canceled. Another time my order for a few bags of fertilizer was changed to a truckload dumped in my garden area. They called it the Stink Garden. Can you even imagine?" she gasped out with disgust.

Vicky was trying very hard to keep a straight face, but Roxanne continued to talk about the Stink Garden, which was making it very difficult. She interrupted Roxanne.

"I'm very sorry for all the trouble that you've had," Vicky said. "I can assure you that we would never allow that to happen here. I have the perfect room for you, and it will be ready within ten minutes, okay?"

"Yes, thank you," Roxanne sighed with relief. "I bet it was Lauren," she muttered under her breath.

"We have a restaurant right over there, why don't you order something while you wait, let the waitress know that it's on the house," Vicky smiled, hoping to cheer the woman up.

"That sounds good," Roxanne nodded and walked over to the restaurant. Vicky picked up the phone and paged the housekeeper on duty. She was a new hire, but had proven herself over the past few weeks while they prepared for the busy weekend.

"Linda, I need room 307 prepared for a guest as quickly as possible," she said.

"No problem," Linda replied swiftly. "I will ring you when it's ready."

"Thank you, Linda," Vicky smiled and hung up the phone. Ten minutes later the phone rang.

"It's ready," Linda said cheerfully when Vicky answered.

"Thanks again," Vicky said and hung up the phone. She walked over to the restaurant to find that Roxanne had Chef Henry's full attention.

"Yes, I grow all of my own herbs to cook with," Roxanne explained. "Anything in a package has lost all of its flavoring."

"It's so frustrating," Chef Henry agreed. "I have a small herb garden behind the kitchen, and it is always nice to be able to go pluck my seasoning fresh off the stem."

"I can really taste it," Roxanne said in a complimentary tone.

"Well, good luck in the contest," Chef Henry said. "I'll be cheering for you!"

"Thanks," Roxanne replied with a smile. Vicky had to wonder why Roxanne was treated so poorly, she seemed to be quite kind.

"Ms. Duran, your room is ready," Vicky said as she walked up to her. "I can take you upstairs if you like."

"No, just leave the key here," Roxanne said. "I can find my way. Thanks."

"You're very welcome, and if you need anything just let us know," she smiled and set the room key down beside Roxanne's plate.

The rest of the afternoon went quickly with Vicky shuttling guests up and down the elevator and Sarah switching rooms and tending to extra accommodation. They both took customer service very seriously. By the time they had dinner that night for the contestants and any guests that wanted to join in, Sarah and Vicky were worn out. Vicky still managed to offer a little help in the kitchen cleaning up. When she left the kitchen and stepped into the empty lobby she sighed with relief.

Sarah was still standing behind the front desk.

"I'm so glad everyone is finally settled in," Sarah said with a sigh when she saw Vicky. She tucked some paperwork into the drawer in the desk.

"Me too," Vicky agreed and glanced out at the empty patio beside the pool. "Do you have enough energy left for a glass of wine?" she asked.

"That sounds wonderful," Sarah smiled and walked around the side of the desk. "I'll get some."

"No, you go sit, I'll get some," Vicky gave her sister's shoulder a light pat.

She walked into the restaurant which had a small bar. Sarah stepped out onto the patio to wait for her. Vicky grabbed a bottle, two glasses and a corkscrew. Then she joined her sister on the patio.

"This is nice," Sarah sighed as she sank down into her chair. She smiled up at the stars spread across the sky.

"How long has it been?" Vicky asked as she opened the bottle of wine.

"Since I had a glass of wine and relaxed?" Sarah asked with a slight laugh. "I can't keep track."

"I think this is the first time you've been away from the kids overnight, isn't it?" Vicky asked and poured them each a glass of wine.

"Yes," Sarah nodded. "It's funny, I thought it would bother me, but I know that Phil is taking good care of them."

"It's nice to be able to trust someone that much," Vicky said. She sat down across from her sister and glanced up at the stars as well.

"He's really great with them," Sarah admitted. "In some ways he reminds me of Dad. He's just very playful."

"Dad was always getting us into trouble," Vicky recalled with a fond smile.

"I know," Sarah giggled. "But he always made sure he told Mom it was his fault."

"You remind me of Mom," Vicky said then took a sip of her wine.

"Thanks, I think," Sarah grinned.

"I mean, you're so loving with the kids, and you always put them first. Mom was like that, too," Vicky smiled.

"She was," Sarah said sadly. "I still miss them."

"Me too," Vicky admitted.

"Is that part of the reason that you are dragging your feet on the wedding date?" Sarah asked. She hid her face quickly with a sip of wine.

"The date, the date," Vicky rolled her eyes and leaned back in her chair. "That's all I hear about."

"I'm just curious," Sarah said quickly. She paused a moment and then looked into Vicky's eyes. "I know it must be hard to think of getting married without them here."

"You know, I never thought it would be a problem, because I didn't think I saw a wedding in my future," Vicky smiled sadly. "But now that I do, yes I do wish they could be here."

"I think that they will be," Sarah said quietly, "just in a different way."

"Maybe so," Vicky agreed and took another sip of her wine. "I sometimes wonder what our lives would be like if they were still here."

"Me too," Sarah admitted. "Neither of us planned on running the inn."

"No, but it has been great to work with you," Vicky said warmly. "It's funny how life seems to make its own plans."

"That's for sure," Sarah agreed. "I just hope life keeps things smooth this weekend."

"So far, so good," Vicky said and raised her glass. Sarah picked up hers and clinked it lightly against Vicky's.

"I'll drink to that," she said with a short laugh and then sipped her wine.

Vicky was silent for a few moments, then sat up in her chair. She leaned a little closer to Sarah.

"What's it like?"

"What's what like?" Sarah asked and looked back at her.

"Marriage," Vicky said and sipped her wine.

"Well, every marriage is different," Sarah pointed out. "It does take some getting used to. Sharing your space with someone, sharing your life with someone."

"How did you know that you were ready?" Vicky asked curiously.

"Honestly, I just hated being away from him," Sarah replied. "When my space felt empty without him, when my life felt lonely without him, I knew that it was time."

Vicky smiled thoughtfully at that. It was like Sarah was putting words to what Vicky had been feeling lately. The room that she had converted into a large apartment in the inn, was home to her. But now, all she could think of was what it would be like to lay down beside Mitchell and to wake up in the morning next to him. She was beginning to feel as if she was counting down the minutes until the next time she would see him.

"I guess that means I'm ready," Vicky said in a murmur.

"Really?" Sarah squealed with excitement. "Can we go dress shopping?"

"No," Vicky said firmly. "I don't think I'm that ready, yet."

"Maybe we should let Aunt Ida pick it out?" Sarah teased.

"Oh my, that would be interesting," Vicky giggled. "I'm sure she would have a ball."

"What about location?" Sarah asked, obviously excited that the wedding might happen soon.

"I haven't really discussed it with Mitchell," Vicky admitted. "But I've planned so many weddings here, I couldn't imagine having it anywhere else."

"I was hoping that you would say that," Sarah said gleefully. "I can't wait!"

"Well, being ready doesn't mean that I've set a date," Vicky reminded her. "I just need to make sure I know what I'm getting myself into."

"You can forget about that," Sarah said with a laugh. "There's no way to know what you're getting into. You just have to trust and jump in."

Vicky grimaced, "That doesn't sound very simple."

"It's actually the simplest thing you can do," Sarah pointed out. "If you think about it and think about it, if you wait for everything to be perfect, it will never happen."

"Hmm," Vicky took the last sip of her wine. "I guess you're right. I hadn't thought about it that way."

"I couldn't think of a more perfect match for

you," Sarah admitted. "We'll have law enforcement in the family!"

"With Aunt Ida around we might just need it," Vicky grinned and took Sarah's glass which was empty. "Want some more?" she offered.

"I better not," Sarah shook her head. "I want to be sharp in the morning."

"Me too," Vicky agreed. "I'll take care of this, you get to bed."

Sarah yawned. "Good idea."

"Night, Sis," Vicky said as she collected the bottle of wine.

"Night," Sarah called back and stepped into the inn.

Chapter Three

The next morning the contest started at nine o'clock sharp and Vicky was ready for it. She had her dark brown hair pinned back and her work jeans on. She wouldn't look dazzling for the camera but that didn't really interest her. What she wanted was to share the experience with Mitchell. She was hoping he would be able to get some time free from work. After recently being promoted to detective his caseload had increased.

Vicky was accustomed to living alone so it didn't really bother her that he had very little free time, but she enjoyed his company so much that when he was gone she was beginning to count the hours until she would see him again. After getting engaged, something she hadn't expected to want, she wasn't ready to face another big change by getting married so soon. It wasn't that she didn't want to marry Mitchell, she did. She was madly in love with him and couldn't imagine ever being with anyone else, she just didn't want to rush into the title of 'Wife'.

A part of her worried that Mitchell would see her differently once they were married. With things going so very well, she didn't feel the urgency to change things. Soon the activity of the morning distracted her from thoughts of Mitchell. There was a festive feeling in the crisp morning air. All the contestants were gathered together in front of the gardens. The host of the contest, Ray Baxter, was standing on the make-shift stage in front of them. Vicky was relieved to see that he didn't expect her to join him.

"Welcome, welcome, to the annual Garnish your Garden contest," he said in a jovial tone.

The crowd of onlookers that had gathered began to applaud and cheer. The contestants were all smiles.

"Today we're going to see what these talented

gardeners can do with their green thumbs. Each contestant will have all day today, and four hours tomorrow to work on their gardens. Not a minute longer. At the end of the contest we will have a chance to look at their creations. We will select three judges from the crowd, and one expert judge, that is, me," he grinned. "Then we will crown the winner and have a nice big party to celebrate. So, who is ready for the contest to begin?" he shouted across the crowd.

The crowd cheered happily and the contestants clapped. Margaret was bouncing up and down, barely able to contain her excitement. Roxanne was already eyeing the available garden space. Lauren had her eyes closed as she drew a few deep breaths. Baron was the only one who looked completely relaxed, with his long arms folded casually across his chest.

"Okay then, on your marks, get set, garden!" Ray shouted and then blew a loud whistle to signal that the contest had begun.

Lauren bolted for the first garden space, the same one that Roxanne was trying to get to.

"I got here first," Lauren shouted as soon as Roxanne set foot in the space.

"No, I did," Roxanne shouted back.

Ray Baxter grimaced and spoke quietly to one of the attendants of the contest.

"If you don't move your big, old foot out of my garden I am going to move it for you," Lauren hissed far more violently than Vicky expected.

"It's staying right there, Lauren," Roxanne said and crossed her arms. "Fair is fair, after all."

"How is it fair that you're trying to steal my garden space?" Lauren demanded with mounting frustration.

"Ladies, I'd like to point out that there is still one more garden space available," the contest attendant said warmly as he paused beside them. "No need to squabble over one patch of land."

"But this one has better lighting," Lauren protested, determined not to move.

"No amount of lighting is going to help your garden," Roxanne muttered under her breath.

"What? What was that?" Lauren demanded, getting irate.

"They're all the same, would you two just pick one each so I don't have to hear you yammering all day?" Baron asked with annoyance.

"Be quiet," Lauren spat at him. "You already have your space. You don't have anything to be upset about."

"Look honey, big bad hubby can't buy you everything," Roxanne teased and wiggled her eyebrows.

Lauren's cheeks were getting red from how angry she was. Vicky knew that things were only going to get worse.

"Isn't there some way we can solve this?"

Vicky asked. She didn't like waiting on the sidelines watching the contest fall apart before her eyes.

"Nothing will make me budge from this spot," Roxanne said stubbornly.

"I'm not going to give up my space," Lauren said firmly.

"She's not very good at sharing," Margaret warned from the garden she had selected. "You two just keep squabbling, while Baron and I set up our gardens and win the contest."

Lauren huffed as she glanced at her watch. "That's the whole plan, isn't it Roxanne, to make me lose?" she growled.

"Oh yes, my life is built entirely around you, Lauren. I'm not the one that tries to get people's names removed from the registry of the contest," she glared at Lauren.

"You're not making any sense," Lauren protested. But she was getting more and more frustrated.

"Listen, the other garden does get beautiful morning light," Vicky said. She felt a little responsible. She had been the one to set up the garden spaces to begin with.

"Move!" Lauren suddenly shouted and barreled into Roxanne. Roxanne was so caught off guard by the screaming that she fell backwards and out of the garden.

"Lauren!" Vicky shrieked and jumped between the two women. "Stop this right this instant!"

"I'm going to have to dock points if this continues," Ray Baxter warned. "Ladies, this is for entertainment, and it is not supposed to be a full contact sport."

"She is the problem!" Lauren nearly screamed.

Vicky helped Roxanne to her feet. Roxanne dusted off her jeans and glowered at Lauren.

"It's fine, I'll take the other garden," she said. "Let the bully win, she always does, one way or another."

She stalked over to the yet unclaimed garden. Vicky was looking between the two with shock. She hadn't expected fighting to break out.

"Good," Lauren said sharply. She picked up the pitchfork that she had brought with her and began clearing her space.

"That was crazy," Vicky said as she walked over to Ray.

"That's gardening," Ray smirked. "Contest style."

Vicky was still shaking her head when she heard someone walk up behind her.

"Morning," Mitchell said warmly and hugged her from behind. Vicky smiled broadly at his warmth around her, and the scent of his cologne.

"You just missed a fight," Vicky said with a

slight giggle.

"What?" he pretended to be disappointed. "And I didn't even get to cuff anyone."

"Well, you wouldn't have wanted to cuff this one," Vicky said in a whisper. "She's Lauren Thomson, Vaughn Thomson's wife."

"The Vaughn Thomson?" Mitchell asked with surprise. "He's here?"

"Right over there," Vicky tilted her head towards a table with an umbrella where Vaughn was seated. He had big sunglasses on. Vicky suspected he was sleeping behind them.

"Yup, that's him all right," Mitchell shook his head with obvious disgust.

"I thought you would be impressed?" Vicky asked as she turned to look at him.

"I can't say that there's much about that man that impresses me," Mitchell admitted. "There's just something about him that has left me unsettled from day one."

"Hmm," Vicky looked back in Vaughn's direction. "He certainly doesn't treat his wife very well."

"Oh?" Mitchell frowned. "There's no excuse for that."

"Hmm," Vicky smiled as she looked into his eyes. "Good to know."

"You already know it," he grinned and kissed her lightly on the lips. "I can't stay long," he frowned. "But call me if another fight breaks out."

"You'll be the first call I make," Vicky promised him and hugged him goodbye. Luckily the rest of the day went fairly smoothly until they had a break for dinner. Vicky had set up a family style dining room for the contestants and the people who were running the contest. That was before she knew about the level of tension that would exist between them. She was nervous as she sat down to dinner with everyone. It started off well with Sarah asking people to share stories of their favorite gardens. But as the dinner wound down, the strangest thing sparked off a volatile rivalry.

"Pass the rolls please," Lauren said begrudgingly to Roxanne. Roxanne had her hand in the bowl and was taking the last roll out of it.

"Sorry, last one," she said without even bothering to look in Lauren's direction.

"Oh, I'm sure we have more in the kitchen," Vicky offered, but her voice was drowned out by Lauren's quick comeback.

"Just like you to be so greedy," she snapped. "You always want to take everything that's mine."

"Lauren, you're nuts," Roxanne said dismissively. Then with her eyes locked on Lauren's she took a big bite of the roll.

"Unbelievable!" Lauren cried out. "You are so rude," she snatched up her purse to leave. When she did Vaughn reached up to stop her. In the process Lauren dropped her purse and the contents spilled all over the floor.

Roxanne and Margaret scrambled to help clean up the mess. Vicky was a little surprised that Roxanne would help, but then she had shown how kind she was to Chef Henry. Vicky picked up the last of the items that had fallen to the floor and handed them to Lauren. Everyone else was looking on in shock.

"Lauren, I'm sorry, I can get more rolls if you would like," Vicky offered swiftly.

"It's not about the rolls!" Lauren huffed. "Why can't anyone see that?" she stalked out of the dining room with Vaughn trailing behind her. After that, the dinner ended quickly.

Vicky decided to check on the floor where Lauren and Roxanne were staying to make sure that they hadn't continued their fight. When she stepped off the elevator into the hallway, she heard a sound that caught her attention. It was the sound of one of the door handles in the hallway rattling. She narrowed her eyes as she noticed Roxanne standing a few doors away. She cringed, as she knew if anything happened to Roxanne it would only make the bumpy start to her stay worse.

"Is anything wrong, Roxanne?" she asked as she paused beside the woman.

"This key isn't working," Roxanne said with frustration.

"Oh, let me take a look," Vicky said and accepted the key when Roxanne handed it to her. "Yes, it looks like there's a problem," Vicky said with some confusion. "This key isn't working because it doesn't belong to this room, it's a key to the Thomsons' room," she shook her head. "How did you end up with this?"

"Oh, I," Roxanne was flustered for a moment before she cleared her throat. "I must have picked up the wrong key at dinner. When we had that little spat over the dinner roll."

"What is it between the two of you?" Vicky asked gently. "How long has this feud been going on?"

"To be honest it started out as friendly rivalry. But it has progressed to become much more intense," Roxanne explained. "But really, I just feel very sorry for her," she said with a sigh.

"Here, let me get this open for you," Vicky offered and used the manager's key so that the door would open.

"Thanks, Vicky," Roxanne smiled.

"I'll just take the key back to Lauren," Vicky added.

"Oh, I wouldn't do that, Lauren doesn't like surprises," Roxanne said before disappearing into her room.

Vicky started to walk down the hall towards Vaughn and Lauren's room to return the key anyway, but she stopped halfway. She really didn't want to aggravate the woman more. She decided to just take the key back to the desk for the night. When she reached the front desk, Vaughn was waiting for her.

"I need an extra key for the room," he said with annoyance in his gaze. "My wife lost hers."

"I found it," Vicky smiled and handed him the key. "Is everything okay, Mr. Thomson?"

"Please, call me Vaughn," he said warmly. "Everything is fine. My wife just gets a little wound up during these contests."

"I understand," Vicky nodded. "Is she resting now?"

"Oh no, she's in the garden," he said. "She'll work all night if she has to."

"That's some dedication," Vicky said with admiration.

"You could call it that," Vaughn said slowly.

"Or you could call it obsession."

Vicky was silenced by his words. Luckily he walked away without expecting her to say anything else. She felt very uneasy when she went to bed that night. She hoped the contest the next morning would be much more pleasant. She set her alarm to get up early and make sure that everything started out smoothly.

Chapter Four

When Vicky woke up the next morning, she did her best to have a good attitude. It was the last day of the contest and she was looking forward to seeing the completed gardens. After she dressed she stepped out onto the patio beside the pool to get some fresh air before breakfast. She was almost immediately greeted by Mitchell.

"You're up early," he said with a grin.

"You're here early," Vicky replied and hugged him.

"Would you believe Sheriff McDonnell insisted I come over here and make sure that everything was going well for Vaughn Thomson?" he raised an eyebrow.

"Ah, so Vaughn does have an admirer on the Highland Police Force," Vicky grinned.

"Maybe just one," Mitchell scowled.

65

"Apparently they are old friends."

"That doesn't surprise me," Vicky laughed a little. Vicky was just about to say something more, when her attention was drawn elsewhere. There was some huffing and grunting coming from the path beyond the pool. A little alarmed by the sound, she glanced at Mitchell.

"Do you hear that?" she asked.

"Yes," he replied and narrowed his eyes. His hand rested lightly on the holster of his gun as he began walking towards the sound. Vicky followed close after him. As they rounded the corner, Vicky had to dodge out of the way as a bicycle came rolling down the path. Mitchell managed to grab it. There was no one riding the bicycle, just the bicycle itself. Chasing after it, with another bicycle in tow, Aunt Ida was huffing and grunting.

"Aunt Ida?" Vicky said with disbelief and hurried over to help her. "What are you doing?"

Ida took a few deep breaths as Mitchell

wheeled the other bicycle back over to her.

"I bought these bikes for Rex and me. I was just going to put them in the garden shed until later this morning," she explained breathlessly.

"You could have asked me to help," Vicky frowned as she looked over her aunt with concern.

"The whole point of all of this is to get into shape," Ida pointed out. "So, I thought I could do it on my own. But that one got away from me," she pointed at the bicycle that Mitchell was holding onto.

"They can be sneaky," he said with a light wink.

"Let us put them away for you," Vicky said with a slight shake of her head. "I don't know if cycling is the right sport for you, Aunt Ida. Aren't you afraid that you'll hurt yourself?"

"Just what are you implying, Vicky?" Ida asked with her shoulders straight and her eyes narrowed. "I have a black belt but you think I'm not capable of riding a bicycle?"

"No, not at all," Vicky back pedaled and Mitchell took the other bicycle from her.

"I'll just put these away," he said casually. Vicky knew he was trying to escape the tension of the conversation.

"I'm just saying that with your age and..."

"Vicky," Ida said sharply. "I'd expect this kind of talk from your sister, because Sarah always thinks she knows best, but you know better than to tell me I can't do something."

Vicky grimaced. "You're right I do," she said. "I'd just hate to see you push yourself a little too hard and end up breaking something."

"Listen to me, young lady, you may think that you're in your prime, but there's not a bone in this body that isn't still strong and ready to be active," Ida lectured sharply. "I can do anything I put my mind to, and I'll thank you to keep your opinions to yourself."

"I'm sorry, Aunt Ida," Vicky said softly. "I didn't mean to say that you're..."

"Old?" Ida supplied with a shake of her head. "Age is a state of mind, Vicky, and I'll prove it." Aunt Ida was well into her seventies but preferred to act like she was in her twenties.

"I'm sure you will," Vicky nodded with a smile of pride. "Nothing has ever been able to stop you."

"Nothing ever will," Ida agreed as Vicky saw Rex walking down the hill to join them.

"I'm sorry if I offended you," Vicky added with genuine remorse. "I just don't ever want to see you get hurt."

"I know, sweetheart," Ida replied in a milder tone. "I'm sorry for coming across so harsh. It's just that Rex tried to use the same argument with me, and it really ruffled my feathers. I want to get fitter, healthier, not waste away from boredom."

"Morning," Rex called out as he joined them.

"Morning," Aunt Ida and Vicky said with a smile.

"Rex and I decided no more motorcycles, only bicycles!" Ida said with determination.

"Really?" Vicky asked as she looked up at Rex with surprise. She knew how much he adored his motorcycle.

"For now," he replied with a frown.

Vicky had to smile a little at how much Rex was willing to sacrifice in order to make Aunt Ida happy, but she was also a little worried that her aunt was asking too much.

"Why don't you two have some breakfast?" Vicky suggested. "I know that Chef Henry has whipped up something special this morning."

"Sounds lovely," Ida agreed. "Do you think Mitchell can handle those bikes okay?"

"Yes, Mitchell will be fine," Vicky promised her with a grin. A few moments after Rex and Ida ducked into the restaurant, Mitchell popped out from behind the shed.

"Vicky," Mitchell called out as he began walking back quickly towards her. Vicky could tell from the look in his eyes that something was wrong.

"What is it, Mitchell?" she asked as she walked towards him.

"Don't go back there," he warned and grabbed her gently by the elbows. "I've already called for backup."

"What? Why?" Vicky asked, her heart beginning to pound. "What's back there?"

"Someone is dead, Vicky," Mitchell said, his eyes dark with concern.

"Let me past," Vicky insisted and tried to pull away from him.

"Trust me, you don't want to see this," Mitchell said gruffly.

"Mitchell, I'm not a child," Vicky growled in return. "This is my inn, I need to know what happened."

Mitchell locked his jaw for a moment, and then reluctantly released her. He took her hand in his and led her around the shed. Vicky gasped when she saw Roxanne's body behind the shed, with a pitchfork sticking up out of her chest.

"Oh no," Vicky moaned. "Are you sure she's dead?"

"Yes," Mitchell frowned. "I checked. It seems like she's been dead for at least a few hours."

"Oh, this is not good," Vicky groaned and crouched down beside Roxanne. "This poor woman."

"Come away from there, Vicky," Mitchell requested sternly. "You don't want to contaminate the crime scene."

"What are we going to do?" Vicky frowned. "We'll have to cancel the contest and send everyone home. I'll go tell Ray Baxter," she said quickly, feeling dizzy from the shock of seeing the body.

"No, you won't," Sheriff McDonnell said as he walked around the back of the shed. "Mitchell, I need to speak with you, now," he said and passed an impatient gaze over Vicky.

Vicky eyed him for a moment. Sheriff McDonnell had a love hate relationship with Mitchell and he made no secret of it, his dislike for Mitchell often extended to Vicky as well. He was more surly than usual this morning.

"Yes sir," Mitchell said gravely and nodded to Vicky. "I just need a minute, darling, okay?"

"Okay," Vicky replied, still stunned. As she stepped out from behind the shed she heard the sound of more sirens approaching. She saw Ray Baxter stepping out of the side door of the lobby with a look of confusion. He glanced at Vicky, but before he could speak, he was waved over by

Sheriff McDonnell. Vicky was slightly relieved. She wasn't sure if she could speak clearly even if she tried. She made her way towards the closest bench in the garden. A few minutes later, Vaughn Thomson emerged from the lobby. He looked troubled as he jogged over to Sheriff McDonnell. Vicky was still in a daze. She pulled out her cell phone and sent a text to Sarah, letting her know that there was an emergency.

Ray Baxter, Sheriff McDonnell, Vaughn Thomson, and Mitchell all stood in a tight knot beside the shed. The crime scene had been roped off by the other officers who arrived, to prevent anyone from treading on evidence. The men were talking in very low voices. Vicky couldn't just sit still any longer. She wanted to know what they were talking about. She didn't want to upset Mitchell, but she was concerned about what was being discussed. Vicky kept inching closer, hoping to overhear what was being said. Before she could listen in too much, Sarah walked right up to her, grabbed her by the arm and tugged her into the middle of the group of men.

"Sarah, wait," Vicky started to say, but Sarah refused to even look at her. She looked determined.

"Sarah, just give us a minute," Mitchell requested and looked nervously from Sarah to Vicky.

"I will not," Sarah replied sternly. Vicky was a little startled by Sarah's bold behavior. "I don't understand why there is a discussion taking place that doesn't involve us, the owners of the inn," Sarah said. "I want to know what has happened."

Mitchell grimaced. "Unfortunately, Roxanne Duran has been found dead behind the garden shed," he said as calmly as he could.

"What?" Sarah blinked, shocked by the revelation. She looked over at Vicky, and Vicky nodded, still not ready to speak about what she had seen.

"This is terrible," Sarah cringed. "We'll have to notify her family. I'm not sure if she left any contact information when she registered."

"We can take care of that," Sheriff McDonnell assured her. "But this is a very delicate matter."

"Of course it is," Sarah said. "We should notify the guests. How did she die? Was it an accident?"

"No," Vicky said and shook her head. "It was no accident."

"So, what are you planning to do about it?" Sarah asked grimly.

"Listen, we're just talking about how to approach this case," Sheriff McDonnell said casually. "It's nothing that you need to bother yourself with."

"Bother myself with?" Sarah asked sharply. Now Vicky's shoulders were up, and her eyes were narrowed. Mitchell had gone a little pale as he stood between the sheriff and his fiancée, as well as his future sister-in-law. "It is entirely my business," Sarah snapped. "This is our property, these are our guests, and I want to know what you're planning on doing about this terrible crime."

"Well, wait just a minute now," Sheriff McDonnell said quickly. "We don't even know that we have a crime..."

"What?" Vicky gasped as she looked at the Sheriff. "Why would there be a body if there is no crime?"

"Maybe the young woman had a little too much to drink," Vaughn suggested. "Alcohol and a pitchfork are not always a good combination."

Sarah stared at him with disbelief and disgust. Vicky crossed her arms, her lips set in a stern, thin line.

"Are you seriously trying to make a joke about a woman who was murdered?" Vicky asked in a grating voice.

"Mitchell, could you explain to your fiancée

that a crime is not a crime just because she thinks it is," Sheriff McDonnell said gruffly and averted his gaze from the two women.

Mitchell's eyes widened, his lips moved soundlessly for a moment. Vicky could tell that he was trying to restrain himself. He looked over at Vicky. Vicky looked back at him, her eyes narrowed as she waited to see if he would follow orders.

"Ah, no, I can't do that," Mitchell said and cleared his throat. His cheeks were red, and his brow was furrowed.

"Excuse me?" Sheriff McDonnell demanded impatiently. "Are you ignoring a direct order?"

"No disrespect, Sheriff McDonnell," Mitchell said calmly. "But there were clearly defensive wounds on the woman's body. She tried to get away from whoever hurt her. Being drunk doesn't cause those kinds of injuries. I'm sure that the Medical Examiner will agree with me," he lowered his eyes briefly before looking back up at Sheriff McDonnell. "I think Sarah and Vicky need to be informed of exactly what is going on."

"Huh, well, I guess I wasn't fully informed," Sheriff McDonnell said with annoyance. It was clear that he was trying to cover up for his initial reaction. "Either way, we're going to keep this quiet. We don't know who has done this, but we can't assume that everyone is in danger. The contest is bringing a lot of interest and tourists into Highland, I don't think we need to cancel it before we know all of the facts. If we move too fast, we might spook the killer, and that could lead to chaos, or never solving this case."

"So, you think it's better that we put our guests and the contestants at risk?" Sarah asked and shook her head.

"I think it's better if we follow the Sheriff's lead," Vaughn said coolly as he studied Sarah intently. Vicky shifted uneasily from one foot to the other. She was usually the one being bold, and getting into trouble. It was unusual for Sarah to be so aggressive.

"I'll do that," Sarah nodded as she looked between the three men. "But you need to find out who did this, and fast," her eyes fell on Mitchell last. "I trust that you will look into this, Detective."

"I will," he promised her and held her eyes for a moment.

"Then it's settled," Ray Baxter said and exhaled. "The contest will continue as planned."

"I don't think that's best," Sarah said with a frown. "But I will do as you ask. If someone else gets hurt because of this, it's your responsibility."

"Of course," Sheriff McDonnell replied. "Now, let us do our work, so that this can be taken care of quickly."

Sarah still looked very annoyed as she steered Vicky back to the bench where she had been sitting.

"Vicky, you look pale," she said gently. "Do you need anything? Water? Do you want to go lay down?"

"No," Vicky said and shook her head. "I just want all of this to be over. I can't believe this happened."

"Well, we're going to have to figure out how to handle this," Sarah frowned. "I feel terrible about not telling the guests and other contestants."

"Me too," Vicky rubbed her cheeks slowly. "But let's allow Sheriff McDonnell and Mitchell to figure something out. If they don't get anywhere, we'll tell the guests ourselves."

"I agree," Sarah nodded. "Why don't you come inside with me?" she suggested.

"I think I just want to wait and talk to Mitchell," Vicky said.

"Okay," Sarah sighed as she saw some of the

guests making their way towards the restaurant. "I'm going to have to tell them something. They will see the police everywhere."

"Just tell them that there was an emergency on the property," Vicky suggested. "Until we find out a little more, that will have to do."

"All right," Sarah tucked her hands into her pockets and walked back towards the inn.

As Vicky sat alone on the bench she felt panic surging through her. She stared at the garden in front of her. It was Lauren's garden. The breeze tickled lightly across the blossoms that had been arranged perfectly throughout the garden. Vicky had never seen such an assortment of colors placed so perfectly that each color accentuated the next. Lauren had labeled it the Rainbow Garden, and the name suited it. There were blossoms of every color. Bright red roses. Deep green ferns that matched the grass. Butter yellow daffodils that reflected the shade of the sun. Bright blue cornflowers that stretched upward towards the bright blue sky.

Vicky was lost in thought over what might have happened to Roxanne. She kept replaying in her mind the last moments she had spent with Roxanne. She heard footsteps slowly approaching her. She didn't bother to look up. There was only one person she expected it to be.

"Are you all right?" Mitchell asked as he stepped up beside her.

"Yes, I think so," Vicky murmured without looking away from the flowers. He sat down beside her on the bench. She felt his arm wind around her waist as he pulled her close.

"I'm sorry this has happened," he said gently beside her ear. "There was nothing that you could have done to prevent it."

"I know that," Vicky said with a frown. "In my mind I know that, but she was just here, only hours ago, standing right here. Now she is gone, and it all happened under my roof."

"Did you notice anything strange about Roxanne?" he asked gently. "Anyone arguing with her or anything like that?"

"Only Lauren," Vicky said softly. "She and Lauren were going at it all day yesterday."

"That's right," Mitchell nodded. "The fight I missed."

"I saw her last night when she went to her room," Vicky sighed. "She didn't seem upset, but maybe a little bothered."

"Did she mention anything about someone looking for her?" he asked.

"No, nothing like that," Vicky replied. "I've been racking my brain, but I can't think of anything out of the ordinary. Who would do this?"

"That's what I'm going to find out," Mitchell said with confidence. "Try not to worry too much," he kissed her forehead. Vicky nodded. She watched as he walked back over to the crime scene. She knew that he would do his best, but she couldn't help wondering whether she had missed something. Had there been some kind of warning sign that she had overlooked?

Chapter Five

Once Vicky had calmed down and the reality that someone had been murdered on the property had sunk in she stood up from the bench and looked out over the gardens. She wasn't going to let anything stop the success of the show, and she certainly wasn't going to allow any more of her guests to die. She could see Mitchell and other police officers fanned out questioning the guests.

Vicky knew that Mitchell preferred her to stay out of his investigations, but this one was too close to home. Besides what harm could a few questions do? She decided to question the staff before they had the chance to speak with the police. She was worried that Sheriff McDonnell was going to inhibit Mitchell's and the other officers' ability to discover the truth. As she stepped into the inn she could see Chef Henry and several of the staff members gathered together near the glass door of the restaurant. She walked towards them. As soon as she reached the door Chef Henry opened it for her.

"Are you all right?" Chef Henry asked with urgency. "I hear that there was a murder, one of the contestants, is that true?"

"It is," Vicky replied grimly. "Which means as of now everyone is a suspect."

"Oh no," one of the waitresses moaned. "This isn't going to be a fun night."

"Just relax," Vicky said calmly. "If you have nothing to feel guilty about then you have nothing to worry about, right?" she looked over the faces of each of the staff members, searching for any hint of deceit. Finding none, she settled her gaze back on Henry. "What I need from all of you is for you to think back over the past few hours. Did anything happen that was unusual? Did something seem out of place? Did you overhear any arguments?" she looked between the faces of the staff. Most of their expressions were blank or thoughtful but no one seemed to be dying to reveal anything.

"Excuse me, Vicky?" Linda asked from the open door of the restaurant. She frowned. "Am I missing a staff meeting?"

"No, it's nothing like that," Vicky assured her. "We're just discussing why the police are here."

"Oh," Linda nodded. She didn't seem very interested in what was happening outside. "I just have a quick question," she said.

"What is it?" Vicky asked. She turned her full attention on the woman.

"I was taking out the garbage in one of the rooms, and I found two used red wine glasses in the trash can. There was nothing else in the trash so should I throw those out, or take them out and wash them? I know every inn does things differently," she frowned nervously.

"We better be safe and throw them away,"

Vicky said with a slight frown. "Who would throw wine glasses out? What room is it? Maybe room service didn't get up there fast enough to retrieve them."

"It was the Thomsons' room," Linda replied.

"Really?" Vicky raised an eyebrow. "And you're sure that there were two wine glasses?"

"I'm sure," Linda nodded. "Do you mind if I wash them and take them home, I always need extra glasses?"

"Sure, go ahead," Vicky nodded. As Linda started to leave the room, Vicky called after her. "Please be careful," she turned back to the rest of the staff. "That goes for all of you. We don't know exactly what is happening here, and until we do, I want you to exercise extreme caution."

"Yes, ma'am," Chef Henry said with a frown. "I'll start by getting those officers some snacks and coffee. That should keep me off the suspect list."

Vicky cringed at his words. "All right everyone, back to work," Vicky said. "Please cooperate with the police and be reassuring to the guests. Let's keep the details of the crime to ourselves for as long as possible. If you notice anyone very upset please report it to Sarah or me as soon as you can."

The staff members nodded before retreating to continue with their duties.

After the staff had dispersed, Vicky was still trying to get things straight in her mind. The two wine glasses in the Thomsons' room really bugged her, because Lauren had made such a fuss about not drinking which had led to a heated moment with Vaughn. So, if the wine glasses didn't belong to Vaughn and Lauren, they must have belonged to Vaughn or even Vaughn and someone else.

Vicky couldn't think of who else that would be. She hadn't noticed Vaughn flirting with anyone. Her staff were strictly ordered not to fraternize with guests, especially married ones. She shook her head and rubbed her eyes. Her head was still spinning from finding Roxanne's body. She stepped out by the pool to clear her head. There were a few officers still conducting interviews but the majority of them had already left.

Vicky wondered if Mitchell was still around. He hadn't said goodbye, so she guessed that he was. Then she thought about Roxanne again. She recalled the last time she had seen her. She had been embarrassed because she had the wrong room key. Vicky drew a sharp breath as she recalled it had been Lauren's room key. Vicky had believed Roxanne when she said that she had picked it up by mistake, but now she wondered. Could she have taken it on purpose? If so, why? Surely it wasn't to sabotage Lauren, that would be a very low move. Was it to share a glass of wine with Vaughn? That seemed odd to her, too, but she thought it was worth exploring.

She went on a hunt for Mitchell. It didn't take her long to find him. He was crouched down beside the shed, studying the ground. The body had already been taken away, likely rushed by Sheriff McDonnell's command.

"Mitchell, I'm glad that you're still here," Vicky said quickly as she walked up to him. "I need to tell you about something."

"I hope it's a lead," he said with a frown as he continued to scrutinize the ground. "Because the one I've got, you're not going to like."

"Well, hear me out," Vicky said swiftly and launched into telling him everything she could about what she had discovered that she thought might be related to the murder. "Last night, when I saw Roxanne for the last time, she was trying to open the door to her room with the wrong key."

"Oh? That's odd," Mitchell agreed. "Maybe they just got mixed up?"

"That's what I thought, but guess whose room

key it was?" she raised an eyebrow.

"Whose?" he asked impatiently.

"Lauren and Vaughn Thomsons'," she replied with a shake of her head.

"Okay," Mitchell nodded. "That's a little odd, but not incredibly so."

"There is one other thing," Vicky said with narrowed eyes. "Apparently someone in the Thomsons' room tried to throw out two wine glasses."

"Why would they throw wine glasses out?" Mitchell asked with confusion.

"That's one question," Vicky nodded. "I also think we need to ask why there were two wine glasses when Lauren doesn't drink," she smiled faintly.

"Oh, so you think Vaughn was in the room with someone else?" Mitchell asked and started to piece things together. "Maybe even Roxanne?"

"I thought maybe it could have been. I don't know what the two of them would be doing sharing wine and it could mean nothing but I thought I had better let you know, just in case."

"I'm glad you did," he agreed with a frown. "Maybe Vaughn threw them out to hide them from Lauren."

"Maybe," Vicky said.

"There's one way to know for sure who drank from the wine glasses. We can check for fingerprints on the glasses to see who was in the room," Mitchell stated.

"Uh oh," Vicky bit into her bottom lip.

"Uh oh, what?" Mitchell asked with a furrowed brow. "You have the wine glasses don't you?"

"I told the housekeeper that she could take them home but she was going to wash them first," Vicky cringed. "Maybe we can still catch her."

"I hope so," Mitchell said as he took off towards the kitchen with Vicky following closely after him. When they reached the kitchen, Linda was there, with a sink full of hot, soapy water.

"Linda," Vicky said out of breath. "Do you still have those wine glasses from the Thomsons' room?"

"Of course I do," Linda nodded and looked warily over at Mitchell.

"Give them to me," Mitchell said urgently.

"Okay, okay," Linda frowned. She dug her hands into the hot soapy water and pulled out two wine glasses. "Do you want to keep them?" she asked.

"There's not going to be anything left on those," Mitchell frowned.

"I'm sorry, Mitchell, I hadn't put two and two together yet, when I told Linda that she could wash them," Vicky frowned.

"Did I do something wrong?" Linda asked, obviously worried.

"No, it's not your fault," Vicky said quickly. "But tell me, did you notice anything else odd about the room? Did it seem like someone else might have been in there?"

Linda thought about it for a moment, with hot water and soap dripping from her fingertips. Then she shook her head.

"No sorry, I didn't notice anything but the wine glasses."

"Without that, I can't do a search of the room," Mitchell frowned.

"Sure you can," Vicky argued. "Why don't you get a warrant?"

"There's no chance of that when it involves the future District Attorney. There's no way that Sheriff McDonnell is going to let me barge in there without more evidence. Not only that, but after the fight I keep hearing about, and Lauren's history with Roxanne, she's currently our prime suspect. Maybe Roxanne and Vaughn were having an affair, and Lauren caught them in the act?"

"In the bed he shares with his wife," Vicky frowned. "That's pretty low."

"Very low," Mitchell said as his cell phone began to ring. Vicky grimaced as she knew the tone belonged to Sheriff McDonnell.

"You better go," she said with a sigh.

"I'll keep you up to date, you do the same," he requested and tapped lightly at his phone.

"Right up to date," she assured him. As he stepped out of the kitchen, Vicky lingered for a moment.

"Linda, do you happen to know if Roxanne was ever in the Thomsons' room?" she asked.

"Actually," Linda wiped her hands on a towel and turned to look at Vicky. "When I was checking out some of the guest rooms I noticed that

Roxanne was in the hallway. I noticed her, because she looked like she didn't want to be seen."

"What was she doing?" Vicky asked anxiously.

"She was just standing there, as if she had no place else to be, tapping a room key against her thigh. I thought it was a little strange because she was standing much closer to the Thomsons' room, than she was her own. I asked if she needed anything, but she said no."

"I see," Vicky nodded. She thought it was very strange, too. So, if Roxanne had known that she had the wrong key the entire time, why did she want it? Why was she trying to get into the Thomsons' room?

Chapter Six

Vicky walked out across the gardens. She could see that the remaining contestants were working hard in their gardens. Vicky couldn't tell if they knew what had happened, but none of the three were willing to stop creating their gardens. Margaret dropped her pitchfork on the sidewalk causing Vicky to jump. The sight of the gardening tool made her flash back to Roxanne's body. She looked back up at Margaret, alarmed. Margaret didn't seem to notice. She fished a candy bar out of her pocket and began unwrapping it. Vicky noticed the bright blue and silver colors of the packaging glistening from the sun, it wasn't a brand she was familiar with.

"This is my last one," Margaret said when she noticed Vicky staring at the candy bar.

"Oh, that's okay," Vicky managed a smile. She turned back to the other contestants. Lauren was crouched down in her garden. Vicky watched Lauren for a long moment. She was pushing mulch around the base of some of her plants. Was Lauren really capable of killing someone? Certainly she had proven that she was violent the day before. If she had been anyone but Vaughn Thomson's wife, she would probably already be in handcuffs. Instead, she was free to work on her garden while the crime was quietly investigated.

Roxanne's garden looked so abandoned compared to the other three. Vicky's mind became sharp as she realized that the best place to look for an explanation about Roxanne's behavior, would be her room. She hurried back into the inn. Sarah was fielding questions from guests in the lobby. She looked a little frazzled as she tried to explain that the police presence did not mean that they were in danger. Vicky snatched the manager's key from behind the counter.

"Do you need my help?" Vicky asked in a whisper when Sarah met her eyes.

"No, I'll be okay," Sarah promised. Then she turned back to answering the questions from the guests.

Vicky rode the elevator up to Roxanne's room. She inserted the key to open the door. Inside there was plenty of evidence that a police search had taken place. There was fingerprint dust everywhere. The bedding had been stripped. Even Roxanne's suitcase had been raided. Vicky stood in the middle of the room for a moment, taking it all in. She wanted to know exactly what Roxanne was doing sneaking into the Thomsons' room. If she was having an affair with Vaughn, Vicky was willing to bet that there was some evidence of her having the affair with her nemesis' husband. Vicky sorted through Roxanne's suitcase first, but she only found what would be expected. She frowned as she knew that if the police had found anything they would have kept it as evidence.

The only way that any evidence of the affair could still be around was if Roxanne had done a really good job of hiding it. She searched under the mattress, then under the bed. As she was climbing back out from under the bed, she noticed that the bedside table was slightly out of place, as if it had been slid forward a few inches. She pulled it out all of the way and a book fell to the floor that had been wedged between it and the wall.

"Yes!" Vicky said and picked up the book. It was a diary. She sat down on the edge of Roxanne's bed and began flipping through the diary. It was filled with thoughts about life and a lot about her gardening. Vicky searched for the last entry in the diary.

Vicky noticed right away that the handwriting had changed from relaxed and loopy to sharp and pressured. She frowned as she read over the last entry which described Roxanne's mounting hatred of Lauren.

I know that she's copying my idea. I knew it

from the moment I heard she was in the contest.
Last year she swore to me that she would ruin
me, all because I had the same color marigolds in
my garden. I think she is going to try to humiliate
me and accuse me of stealing her plans. There's
only one way I can know for sure. I have to get
into her room, and get into her notebooks. If I can
see what she has planned out, then I'll know what
she is up to. I wish I could just enjoy the contest,
instead I'm going to have to play spy.

"So, she did try to sneak into the room," Vicky
said softly. "But not for an affair. She tried to
sneak in because she wanted to find out what
Lauren was planning for her garden." She glanced
down at the last few lines of text at the bottom of
the page. They seemed to be added on as an
afterthought.

I don't know what to do. I've seen too much

now. I don't think I can ever look at Lauren the same way. The poor woman has more troubles than a gardening contest.

Vicky raised an eyebrow at the last remarks. Her stomach flipped with nervousness. What had Roxanne seen that could cause her to go from hating Lauren to feeling pity for her? She wasn't sure what to think, but she was certain it had to be something that Roxanne had seen in that room. If she wasn't having an affair with Vaughn, then who had the other wine glass belonged to? Vicky doubted that he would have invited Roxanne in for a drink, especially if he caught her trying to sneak into his room. Goosebumps rose up along Vicky's arms as she realized that whatever Roxanne might have seen in that room could have been the reason that she had been murdered.

"I've seen too much, now," Vicky repeated in a whisper. She heard footsteps out in the hallway.

Quickly, she tucked the book back behind the bedside table, and pushed the piece of furniture back into position against the wall. She was standing up when Vaughn Thomson filled the doorway of the room.

"Vicky, what are you doing in here?" he asked.

Vicky cleared her throat. "Just checking on things to see if housekeeping can come in and clean up yet."

"Oh," he nodded a little. "Well, I was looking for you. There's only a few hours left in the contest. I'm going to help Lauren a little with her garden. I was wondering if you could bring drinks out onto the patio for all of us."

Vicky nodded. "No problem," she replied with a smile.

Vicky knew that Vaughn could have easily asked anyone in the restaurant. He hadn't been looking for her at all. He was just trying to come up with an excuse for visiting Roxanne's room. As

Vaughn left, Vicky understood what Mitchell had said about the man just rubbing him up the wrong way. If Lauren was the killer then he was obviously interested in protecting her. But no one had been there to protect Roxanne.

Vicky pulled out her phone and placed a call to the restaurant, asking them to bring drinks out to the contestants and their guests. Then she tucked her phone away. She felt as if she was missing something. With her mind trying to work through all of the random evidence that was piling up, Vicky decided that she needed to find more proof to make sense of it. She walked down the hall to the Thomsons' room.

Vaughn had said that they would both be working on Lauren's garden. She was guessing that she was going to have plenty of time to look around. Vicky knocked lightly on the door of their room, and waited. When she received no response, she knocked again, only harder just to be certain. If she was caught breaking into the future District Attorney's room, she would have a lot to answer for. She still didn't hear anything.

Assuming that they were not in the room Vicky used the key to open the door. When she pushed it all the way open she braced herself for the possibility that someone might still be inside. Instead what she found was an impeccable room, with everything put neatly away. Vicky walked over to the bedside table where there were some papers piled up. She began sorting carefully through them so that she would be able to put them back exactly the way she found them. Some were notes for Lauren's garden. Mixed in were a few campaign schedules. Nothing incriminating.

Vicky walked around the bed to the other side. She saw a candy wrapper on the floor but then her attention shifted as she noticed Lauren's suitcase on the floor next to it. She crouched down to open it and have a look inside. Just as she did, she heard the click of the lock on the door being released. Her heart dropped as she realized that someone was opening the door. She was too scared to think straight. She dove under the bed and flattened herself against the floor.

"I was out there to support you," Vaughn said as he stepped into the room.

"You were sipping drinks and flirting with the waitress," Lauren argued. "Is it too much to ask you not do it in public? It's very embarrassing."

"You think being friendly is flirting," Vaughn accused. "How embarrassing do you think it was for me, when you stomped off throwing a tantrum?"

"I do not throw tantrums," Lauren hissed in return.

"Lauren, you've been miserable since we got here. I thought all of this would make you happy," Vaughn exclaimed, obviously frustrated. Vicky heard what sounded like a choking sound. For an instant she wondered if one was assaulting the other, but then she realized it was Lauren trying not to cry. Vicky lay as still and quiet as she could under the bed. She didn't dare to breathe too deeply.

"I can't believe this, I just can't believe it," she heard Lauren say, her voice trembling as she spoke. "This was supposed to be my year, Vaughn. Now everything is ruined. There's no way that the contest will go on with all of this happening."

"That's not true, Lauren," Vaughn said calmly. "Just think of it this way, now you have less competition."

"That's terrible, Vaughn, you shouldn't say that," Lauren chastised. "Roxanne was never competition for me in the first place, you know that."

"Either way, she's no longer an issue," he said. "So, why not just look at it as a gift?"

"A gift, you're sick, Vaughn," Lauren sighed. "Not only is someone dead, but don't think for a second that they aren't going to look at me. I was in a fight with her, they're going to try to pin everything on me."

"Lauren, sweetheart, you're forgetting who you are," Vaughn said arrogantly. "You're my wife. No one is going to pin anything on you. So, just try to relax and enjoy the contest. That's why we came here, right?"

"Don't call me sweetheart," Lauren shot back with annoyance.

"Sorry," Vaughn mumbled.

Vicky could see Lauren pacing back and forth in front of the bed. She cringed when Lauren stopped right beside her and began to speak.

"My only real competition is Margaret," Lauren said. "Of course, she's not going anywhere," she paused a moment. Vaughn was silent. "Don't think I don't see the way she looks at you," she added darkly.

"Can you blame her?" Vaughn asked with a soft chuckle. "I mean, I am handsome."

"You're an arrogant piece of work is what you are," Lauren shot back. "If my parents hadn't pressured me into marrying you..."

"Oh yes, you're really suffering," Vaughn said gruffly. "Is it the luxury car or the mansion with a personal chef that's bothering you, Lauren?"

"Maybe it's the fact that you are too busy patting yourself on the back to realize that a marriage is supposed to be about two people," Lauren shot back.

"Lauren, please," Vaughn said impatiently. "Do we have to do this now? Here?"

"Fine, I'll drop it," Lauren sighed. "It's not like my opinion has ever mattered to you anyway. So, just enjoy your stay at the Heavenly Highland Inn," she stomped towards the door.

"What's that supposed to mean, Lauren?" he called after her. "Don't even think about embarrassing me by trying to get another room. If you can't be mature about this, then the reporters are going to be all over me like flies. I will not lose District Attorney because you wanted to throw a tantrum."

"Don't worry, Vaughn," Lauren said from the doorway. "You'll get your precious District Attorney, but I can't stand to look at you for another second." And with that she closed the door sharply behind her.

Vicky bit her bottom lip. Not only was she afraid to get caught, but now she had learned a lot more about Vaughn and Lauren's relationship than she ever wanted to know. If a marriage could turn into this, it was definitely not for her. She waited patiently, hoping that Vaughn would leave soon. She heard him open a bottle of wine. Then she heard him pour a glass. She closed her eyes briefly, worried that he intended to settle for a while. She was regretting hiding under the bed when she could have just made an excuse for being there. Then she heard him pick up the phone.

"I know, don't worry about that," he said quickly. "Just meet me by the pool."

He paused. She heard him gulp down his wine. "Listen to me, I'm not going to argue with you right now, just meet me by the pool."

Vicky couldn't believe that he had called Lauren to continue the fight. She and Mitchell had their spats, but nothing like this couple. Vaughn hung up the phone. Then he walked towards the door. Vicky was getting ready to slide out from under the bed when her hand brushed across something smooth and square. Carefully and silently she picked up the square tag. She could barely make out the picture and the writing on it. What she saw made her blood run cold.

The door being closed jolted her out of her shock. She held her breath a moment and listened closely. She didn't hear anyone else in the room. Slowly she exhaled and then slid out from under the bed. She kept the tag held tightly in her hand.

When she stood up, she looked at it more closely. As she had suspected it was a tag from the hardware store, for a pitchfork. Her hand was shaking as she tucked it into her pocket. She didn't know how yet, but she was sure that it was connected to the crime.

As Vicky slipped out of the door, she remembered the candy wrapper beside the bed. It had been so familiar to her because Margaret had been eating that same kind of candy bar earlier in the day. Had Margaret been inside the room, too? Was she trying to scope out Lauren's plans as well? Vicky was feeling very confused as she rode the elevator down to the lobby. When she stepped off the elevator, she noticed Ray Baxter talking heatedly to Baron. Vicky did her best to be invisible as she stepped closer to them.

"This is ridiculous. I just heard that Roxanne is dead. How can you continue the contest?" Baron demanded.

"The contest must go on. Roxanne would want it to," Ray pointed out.

"Roxanne would want to be alive," Baron snapped back. "How do I know someone isn't targeting contestants? You saw how crazy Lauren got yesterday. I'm not going to put my life at risk over a contest."

"Calm down, Baron," Ray insisted. "There's no evidence to show that contestants are being targeted. I'll tell you what, we'll take a break. We'll move the last part of the contest to this afternoon and evening, so that the police have the chance to investigate. Will that work for you?"

"I guess," Baron sighed. "I still think it's ridiculous."

"We're just trying hard to deal with an unexpected situation," Ray frowned.

Vicky was relieved to hear that Ray was going to move the last part of the contest to the evening. She knew that once the contest was over several of the guests and all of the contestants would be leaving. That meant witnesses and suspects would vanish before the case was solved.

"I'll gather the other contestants," Baron said. "So that we can all be informed of the change."

"Good," Ray nodded. "I'll make the announcements out by the gardens."

"I'm going to find Sarah," Vicky said quickly. "She'll make an announcement to the guests who are here for the contest."

"Great," Ray nodded. "Hopefully all of this will be settled soon."

As Vicky was walking towards the patio door Aunt Ida and Rex stepped into the lobby.

"Vicky, what's happened?" Aunt Ida asked with concern.

"There's been a murder," Vicky replied as she paused beside the door. "One of the contestants."

"What?" Aunt Ida gasped. "Are you okay, is

Sarah?"

"We're okay," Vicky nodded. "We're just trying to figure out who is responsible for it. Mitchell might want to talk to you and Rex since you were out by the shed this morning."

"Well, we went on our jog," Ida nodded her head. "I don't know what we could tell him."

"Did you see any of the contestants outside or inside the inn this morning?" Vicky asked.

"I did, but not here," Ida snapped her fingers. "We ran around the main strip in town. We saw Lauren Thomson coming out of the hardware store with a pitchfork. I thought it was a little strange, because we have pitchforks here that she could borrow if she didn't have one, but I figured as picky as Lauren seems to be maybe she wanted a certain kind."

Vicky nodded as her mind made the connection between the tag she had found on the floor under the bed in the Thomsons' room.

"I'll let Mitchell know. If you think of anything else, just tell me," she requested.

"We will," Rex nodded. He was drenched in sweat and looked very uncomfortable in his tight clothes.

"Be careful," Ida warned as she looked straight into Vicky's eyes. "Don't you get into the middle of all of this, not unless I'm with you."

Vicky smiled and hoped her aunt couldn't tell that she had already gotten right into the middle of things. Vicky started thinking about why Lauren would buy a pitchfork. Was she overthinking things and she just wanted a new pitchfork, she was a gardener after all? Unless she was intending to replace the one she had used to kill Roxanne. Maybe it was just a coincidence but it seemed like a very strange coincidence.

Chapter Seven

Vicky decided to check out her hunch and check the garden shed to see if she could find if a pitchfork had been replaced. Along the way she stopped at the kitchen to see if Sarah was there. She wanted to keep her informed of what was happening. Sarah was perched on a stool sitting not far from Chef Henry in the kitchen. Chef Henry was bent over a soup he was preparing for the meal that evening.

"Are you hiding out?" Vicky asked as she walked up to her sister with a slight frown.

"Maybe," Sarah replied. "Is that wrong?"

"Not unless you're hiding from me," Vicky nudged her lightly. "I just wanted to let you know that the contest is being delayed for a few hours so that the police have time to conduct their investigation. I told Ray you would announce it to the guests, but if you'd like I'll do it," she offered.

"No, it's fine, I can do a mass call to all of the rooms," Sarah nodded. When she left the kitchen Chef Henry turned towards Vicky.

"This is a little crazy that he still wants to host the contest," he frowned. "Roxanne was a very nice lady."

"Well, she was also trying to break into rooms," Vicky sighed. "I think that there is a lot more to this story than we may ever know."

"That may very well be the case," Chef Henry nodded. "I think it's best if you stay out of the middle of all of this, Vicky."

"Isn't that Mitchell's line?" Vicky grinned, forgetting for a moment all of the turmoil that was occurring.

"I beat him to it," Chef Henry said and pointed his wire whisk at her. "You keep yourself safe."

"I will do my best," Vicky promised. She didn't mention sneaking into two rooms and almost being caught in one of them. By the time she went back outside, Ray was making the announcement to the contestants, who were expecting to begin work on their gardens.

"Unfortunately, because of the circumstances we are faced with today, we are going to need to delay the continuation of the contest for a few hours. We will keep you up to date as to when you can expect to start on your gardens again."

When Vicky looked at the contestants to see their reaction, she was surprised to see that only Baron and Lauren were there. Lauren did not look pleased at all.

"We want to know what's going on here," Lauren explained with impatience. "One minute we have a contest, the next no one even seems to be running it."

"What do you mean?" Vicky asked with concern.

"Well, Margaret hasn't even bothered to show

up," Lauren explained with annoyance. "Who am I supposed to compete with? Baron?" she shook her head and pointed her thumb over her shoulder at his garden. "It's a green and white garden. Who would want a green and white garden? Gardens are supposed to be about color."

"Excuse me, it's called having a different view of life, it's called artistry. It's called being unique, none of which you would know anything about with your glittery hair. Glitter, in your hair, really?" Baron scowled.

"Oh hush, Baron, I'm not worried about your opinion. What we should both be worried about is whether we are going to see this contest finished or if we've wasted all of our time here," Lauren said impatiently.

"Well, considering that there is a lot happening here right now, I think you might understand why things are a little bumpy," Vicky stammered out. She couldn't forget being trapped under the bed earlier in the day, and listening to Lauren and Vaughn have it out.

"A little bumpy?" Lauren shook her head again. "I don't think this is even a real contest anymore."

"It is a real contest," Ray insisted as he stood in front of them. "It has to be. The magazine has invested too much time and money for it to be canceled."

Just then the door leading from the restaurant into the gardens burst open. Sarah came running across the path.

"Good, I sent your sister to see if she could find Margaret," Ray explained.

Sarah stopped breathlessly in front the group. "We have a problem," she said with fear in her eyes.

"Great, not another problem," Lauren rolled her eyes.

"I can't find Margaret. I think she is missing," Sarah said with alarm in her voice.

"Oh no," Ray frowned.

"I better call, Mitchell," Vicky said and pulled out her phone.

"Wait," Ray said quickly. "How do you know she's missing?"

"I just checked in her room. Her purse was there, along with her house keys and wallet. All her clothing is there. But there's no sign of her," Sarah frowned.

"Did you check my husband's bed?" Lauren snorted under her breath. Only Vicky caught what she said.

"Excuse me?" Sarah asked as she looked at her.

"Nothing," Lauren said quickly. "I know she isn't missing. I saw her in the garden before lunch," she shook her head. "She disappeared after we got the news that the contest was going to be delayed."

"When you saw her, did she say anything?" Vicky pressed. She texted Mitchell the information so that she wouldn't have to interrupt the conversation. She was sure that Lauren might be the key, considering that first Roxanne was dead, and now Margaret was missing. Lauren had motive in both crimes. Roxanne was her only real competition, and Margaret was no competition in the garden, but she might certainly be in the bedroom.

"Sure, I was working on my garden. She showed up there, and I thought she was trying to keep up with me. But she just hung out there near the pool," Lauren shrugged. "I asked her if she had heard about the delay. She said she had and told me that she was just trying to have some alone time."

"So, maybe she just wandered off?" Ray

suggested. "Maybe she was trying to kill some time..." he cringed. "Sorry, wrong words to use. But if she wanted some alone time, that might be why we can't find her."

"It doesn't really matter why she's missing, does it?" Lauren snapped. "All that matters is what is going to happen with the contest?"

"Let's just give it an hour or two and we'll see if we can locate Margaret," Ray suggested.

"I'll let the staff know," Vicky said. Just as she was about to head back into the inn she saw Mitchell striding up to the group. Lauren started to walk off back towards her garden.

Vicky opened her mouth to speak to Mitchell, but he brushed right past her and caught up with Lauren. "You need to stay right here with me," Mitchell said sternly. Lauren stared at him with disbelief.

"I can go wherever I please," she said flatly.

"Ma'am, you were seen fighting with the

murder victim, and now we believe that you might have been the last person to see the missing person alive. I need to question you," Mitchell said flatly. Vicky stared at him as he locked eyes with Lauren. When he exercised his authority, she couldn't help but watch. The glint of his eye, the clench of his jaw, and the broadness of his straightened shoulders was enough to intimidate anyone.

"But you don't understand..." Lauren began to say.

"What is going on here?" Vaughn demanded as he walked up to the group. "Lauren? What's wrong?" he asked. "Why hasn't the contest started?"

"Sir, you'll have to step away. This is a murder investigation, and I'm questioning your wife about her involvement," Mitchell turned to face Vaughn without the slightest hesitation.

"Excuse me?" Vaughn said, clearly offended.

"Do you have any idea who I am, Officer?"

"It's detective," Mitchell replied smoothly. "Yes Sir, I know exactly who you are, Mr. Vaughn Thomson. That does not change anything. I need to question your wife about a murder and a missing person."

"That's ridiculous," Vaughn said dismissively. "You're going to find yourself in a world of trouble if you keep up these false accusations," he warned Mitchell.

"I am not accusing anyone. I just need to find out what she knows," Mitchell said through clenched teeth and smiling lips. "Certainly, it isn't the goal of the Highland Police Department to make a future District Attorney uncomfortable. But seeing as you are hoping to be elected into such a powerful position where honesty is of the utmost importance, I would assume that you wouldn't want me to demonstrate any kind of favoritism, would you?"

Vaughn glared openly at Mitchell. Vicky had to bite the tip of her tongue to keep from smirking. She could clearly tell from Mitchell's body language that he was holding in the desire to slap a pair of handcuffs on Vaughn.

"Wait please," Lauren said with a sniffle. "I had nothing to do with any of this. I did see Margaret near the pool today, but she was still there when I left. She was going on about how she wanted to be alone, so I decided to give her some privacy. I went to get something to eat in the restaurant."

"Well, that's easy enough to check," Sarah volunteered. "I can ask the staff members that are working today if they served Lauren."

"I was there for a while," Lauren said tearfully. "I didn't want to go back upstairs," she glanced furtively at Vaughn. Vaughn narrowed his eyes sharply at her.

"We had a bit of a spat earlier today," he

confided to Mitchell. "But I'm sure Lauren had nothing to do with any of this. While you are wasting precious time investigating her, the real murderer is getting away. Don't forget that. You will have that on your shoulders."

Mitchell looked directly into Vaughn's eyes. "Don't worry, Sir, one thing I don't ever forget is a murderer. Your wife is staying right here, until she answers all of my questions. You are welcome to stay with her, if you would like," he smiled again.

Vicky was rather impressed with Mitchell's restraint. She knew from his tensed jaw and the twitch at the corner of his eye that he was quite upset.

"I think I will," Vaughn said grimly. "In fact I'm going to get Sheriff McDonnell over here so that he can witness this as well."

"Fine, I'll call him myself," Mitchell said.

"I'll do it," Vaughn spat back.

While Mitchell was arguing with Vaughn, Vicky had walked over to Sarah.

"This is getting out of hand," she said.

"Yes, it is," Sarah replied. "I think we need to cancel the contest for now. It's clear that the contestants are either being targeted, or something else sinister is going on here. I can't in good conscience allow this to go on."

"You're right," Vicky said in an attempt to be supportive. "I know that Lauren and Baron will be disappointed, but it's our only choice."

"I'll let Ray know," Sarah sighed. "I guess when I said that I hoped that nothing went wrong this weekend, I should have been more specific."

They both watched as Sheriff McDonnell arrived and walked over to Mitchell, Vaughn, and Lauren. Whatever he said must have annoyed Mitchell, because Vicky watched his shoulders tense up beneath his button down shirt. Mitchell shook his head and didn't even attempt to be respectful as he turned and stalked over towards Vicky.

"I'm out of here," Sarah said quickly when she saw Mitchell's angry walk. "I have no interest in getting between a sheriff and his detective."

Vicky gave her a look as if to say, don't leave me here, but Sarah was already gone. Mitchell paused in front of Vicky and shoved his hands deep into his pockets. His cheeks were red with irritation. Vicky cringed at the sharpness of his narrowed eyes.

"Want to walk with me, I am going to talk to the restaurant staff?" Mitchell offered as he looked over at Vicky.

"Sure," Vicky nodded. She wanted to spend time with him, but she was very worried about Margaret.

"Apparently, Lauren claims she was in the restaurant after she saw Margaret by the pool," he said sternly. "So, I am going to verify that that is the case and see if anyone else saw Margaret by pool. Can you get the restaurant staff together for me please?"

Vicky organized it so that Mitchell could interview each of them separately.

Mitchell's expression was grim as he walked back out of the restaurant.

"Well," he sighed. "The waitress confirmed Lauren's presence in the restaurant, but no one else saw Margaret by the pool."

"Maybe she was there but they just didn't see her," Vicky said.

"Maybe," Mitchell frowned. "But it would help verify her story. We need to get to the bottom of this. We have at least one but possibly two victims."

Mitchell's words hit Vicky hard. She knew that he was right. There was no solid suspect.

"Mitchell, the murder weapon. What did it

look like?" she asked.

"What do you mean?" he frowned. "You saw it. It was a pitchfork."

"But did it look like it had been used for a while, or did it look brand new?" she looked at him intently.

"It was pretty beat up," Mitchell said and his frown deepened. "But why does that matter?"

"It matters because Aunt Ida and Rex saw Lauren Thomson buying a brand new pitchfork this morning at the hardware store in town. So, if it isn't the murder weapon, did she buy it to replace the murder weapon, but she didn't get a chance to?"

"That's a stretch," Mitchell winced. "But it's worth looking into."

They walked through the door that led out by the pool. The garden shed was still roped off as a crime scene. Mitchell lifted the yellow tape so that Vicky could duck under. When she opened the door to the shed she was shocked. It looked as if a bomb had gone off in it. There were pots and gardening tools strewn everywhere.

"What's all this?" she asked with disbelief.

"Oh, the officers did a search in here," Mitchell said guiltily. "I guess they were a little messy."

"A little?" Vicky asked as she looked at him with a mixture of annoyance and shock.

"Here, I'll help you straighten up a little," Mitchell offered and began collecting pots off the floor. Vicky sorted through some of the mess as well, but she was looking for pitchforks. She found three of the old beat up pitchforks that they used to tend the gardens but no new ones.

"Looks like I was wrong," Vicky sighed.

"We can't be right all the time," Mitchell said with a sigh. "Even though you usually are."

"I still think that Vaughn is hiding

something," Vicky said.

"I wouldn't put it past him," Mitchell nodded. "Maybe he is trying to cover up for Lauren."

"Maybe," Vicky replied. "Or maybe Lauren tried to help him clean up his own mess and that's why she bought a new pitchfork."

"Any of that is possible," Mitchell agreed. "I still don't understand how Margaret is involved in all of this."

"I'm not sure," Vicky admitted. "But we need to keep a close eye on the Thomsons."

"That won't be a problem," Mitchell assured her. "In fact, I'm going to go take a deeper look into Vaughn and Lauren's background."

"Hopefully it turns up something," Vicky said with a sigh as she looked over the rest of the destroyed shed.

"Don't worry, I'll be back to help you with this," Mitchell said. He stole a light kiss before leaving the shed. Vicky stood there a moment longer, then she heard someone's phone ringing outside of the shed. She froze at the sound of it. She heard Vaughn's voice as he answered it.

"I know, I know, but I'm swamped here right now," he said. His voice was slightly muffled because Vicky was in the shed. Just as it had been when he was talking on the phone in his room earlier. "Don't worry, I'll be back in the office by tomorrow. Everything is fine."

After he stopped talking, Vicky's heart began pounding. She knew he was still standing right outside. Did he know that she was in there listening? She waited until she heard his footsteps walking away from the shed. Nervously she poked her head out of the shed. She couldn't see anyone on the path in front of the shed. She stepped outside slowly. As soon as she was sure she was alone, she took a deep breath to clear her mind. She remembered hearing Vaughn speak on the phone to someone. She remembered him asking that person to meet him by the pool. The last place that Margaret had been seen was by the pool.

Vicky's eyes widened. She ran across the courtyard to the side entrance of the lobby. She burst through the door and ran to the front desk where Sarah was standing.

"Vicky, are you okay?" she asked as she looked up with surprise.

"Can you pull up the call log?" Vicky asked breathlessly. "I need any calls going out from the Thomsons' room."

"Okay," Sarah nodded. She could tell that Vicky was in no mood to explain.

"I have one from a few hours ago," Sarah said.

"Can you tell who it went to?" Vicky asked.

"It wasn't one of the rooms in the inn," Sarah said. "But I can give you the phone number."

Vicky pulled out her cell phone. She dialed the number that Sarah read off to her. At first all it did was ring. Then suddenly she heard a voice.

"Hi, you've reached Margaret, I must be in my garden, so please leave a message," the recording said cheerfully.

Vicky felt sick to her stomach as it confirmed that it was Margaret who Vaughn had called. Margaret had been waiting for Vaughn by the pool. She hung up her phone and dialed Mitchell's number. He had not left that long ago and she hoped that he would be able to get back quickly. Mitchell didn't answer, so Vicky left him a message.

"Mitchell, I know for a fact that Margaret was waiting by the pool for Vaughn," she spoke quickly into the phone as she slipped out of the lobby and back into the gardens. "I think he might have done something to her or maybe Lauren saw them together and lost her temper and did something. Meet me at the inn as soon as you can," she hung up the phone. Her hands were slippery with sweat from the anxiety she felt. She tucked her phone into her pocket, and then turned quickly when she heard a noise behind the garden shed. A moment later a squirrel darted across the grass. Vicky sighed with relief.

Vicky scrutinized the garden area, searching for anything that might be more evidence to use against Vaughn. She knew that the police were doing a good job, but she knew the Heavenly Highland Inn better than they did. She wondered if they had missed something, a clue, or a sign of where Margaret might have been taken. The gardens were quiet, and empty. Everyone else had returned to their rooms to pack or had gone to the restaurant for a final meal.

Vicky was sure that there had to be something to find. She needed something to connect the murder to a suspect. If they had the suspect they might be able to find Margaret. She wanted all of this to be over. She paused at the garden in front of the garden shed, where she knew the first murder had taken place. She could only assume that the murderer had spent some time here, waiting for his opportunity. She bent over in front of the blossoms that were low to the ground. She was determined to find something that could make a solid unquestionable connection.

As she started to stand back up Vicky felt something strange. It was almost as if tiny nails were digging into her back. She started to turn to see what it was, but when she felt the prongs poking through her shirt and into her skin she suddenly knew exactly what it was. Her breath caught in her throat as she froze where she stood.

Chapter Eight

"Walk back towards the shed," a voice from behind Vicky commanded. Vicky recognized it right away. The prongs of the pitchfork poked harder into her back. She reluctantly took a step forward. Her heart was racing. She was suddenly certain that if she went behind that shed she would never come out again.

"No," she said shakily. "I'm not going back there."

"Fine, then I'll make you," the person behind her said. Her arms were grabbed hard behind her. Vicky twisted in an attempt to get away. Instead she was dragged back behind the shed. Roxanne had been killed behind that shed. Would that be her fate, too? She tried to think of a way to escape, but her mind kept flashing back to Roxanne's body laying there with a pitchfork sticking out of it. She didn't want to die that way. When the person finally released her again, she reached for her cell phone which should have been tucked into her pocket. But there was nothing there.

"You're not going to get away with this," she said softly, even though she knew differently.

"I will get away with anything I please," the voice replied. Vicky rounded the corner behind the shed, and felt her muscles tense.

"Just let me go, this doesn't have to happen," she pleaded softly.

"You're right, it didn't have to happen. If you had just stayed out of it, it probably wouldn't have happened. But you had to be nosy, so here we are," the growl of the voice was menacing. Vicky had no doubt that she was in grave danger.

"How can you do this?" she asked incredulously. "You're supposed to protect people."

"I do," the person replied sharply. "I protect the people who deserve protecting."

"Vaughn," she exhaled his name with disgust. Vaughn Thomson had murdered Roxanne. "Where's Margaret?" she asked shakily.

"She's right there," Vaughn replied coldly and tilted his head towards the bushes behind the shed. She had to clamp her hand over her mouth to keep from screaming. The woman's body was well hidden by the brush, but now that she knew where it was, she couldn't look away.

"Shh," Vaughn warned her. "If you scream, I will make sure that your sister Sarah, and your Aunt Ida are next."

Vicky looked up at him with fear in her eyes. There was no question in her mind that he would follow through with his threat. With all of his influence he might never get caught. She was sick to her stomach as she realized there was no way out of this.

"It's nothing personal," he explained when her eyes became moist with tears. "It's just that my career is very important. I'm going to help a lot of people, and I'm going to make a difference in the community."

Vicky was stunned as she realized he really meant what he was saying. He still considered himself a good person, despite the two, soon to be three, people that he had murdered.

"Just let me go, Vaughn," Vicky said swiftly. "You know that no one will believe anything I say. You are who you are, and no one is going to consider you a suspect."

"You're right about that," Vaughn nodded. "But I can't take the risk. I couldn't take the risk when Roxanne caught Margaret and me together in a compromising position. Lauren is already suspicious, and she would be livid if she found out about the affair I was having with Margaret. A scandal like that could have ended my career before it had the chance to begin."

"Roxanne caught you with Margaret?" Vicky

whispered, knowing the woman's body was not far away. That must have been who he shared the glass of wine with. It confirmed that he was on the phone to Margaret when Vicky hid under the bed. So, Vaughn had killed Roxanne to keep her quiet about what she had seen, but that didn't explain Margaret. If Vaughn was having an affair with her, why had he killed her?

"Sure, she's a fine woman. She doesn't complain all the time like Lauren does. She didn't mind being discreet. I'm really going to miss her," he sighed and then shook his head. "Too bad, if Roxanne hadn't broken into our room, none of this would have had to happen."

"I don't understand," Vicky gulped out. "Why didn't you just threaten Roxanne?"

"Roxanne isn't the type to keep her mouth shut," Vaughn explained with annoyance. "I would always have to be blackmailing her or threatening her to keep her quiet. It was really just too much work. So, I grabbed a pitchfork and ended it there and then. I hid the body behind the shed. Once she was dead I was going to replace the pitchfork I had used. But Margaret interrupted me with incessant phone calls. Then she found me walking out from behind the shed. She must have spotted some blood on my clothes," he cringed. "I tried to get her to forget about it, tried to convince her that it was all in her head. But she wouldn't listen, especially after the body was found," he shook his head slowly. "Then she kept saying how it was wrong for me to have killed Roxanne, that she was an innocent woman, blah blah blah," he closed his eyes for just a moment.

"So, you killed her?" Vicky asked in disbelief.

"She was certain that I had killed Roxanne, she was going to go to the police," he frowned. "I couldn't let that happen, now could I?" he asked. "Not after how hard I've worked, how much I've sacrificed."

"Was Lauren involved?" Vicky questioned. "Why did she buy a new pitchfork?"

"I used hers for the murder but she thought she had lost it. She didn't even suspect I had used it," he explained smugly. "She hates sharing so she went to buy a new one. The same one that I am going to use to kill you."

"You are a cruel man," Vicky declared. If she was going to die, she was going to give him a piece of her mind first. "You're terrible to your wife, you murdered two people for no good reason, and you act like taking someone's life is nowhere near as important as your career. You're the criminal that should be locked away, not the one who should be prosecuting criminals."

"Watch your mouth," Vaughn warned and pushed the pitchfork harder against her. "I can make this quick or slow."

There were footsteps and voices in the distance. Vicky took a deep breath as Vaughn glared at her. She knew that if she cried out, the prongs of the pitchfork would be pushed into her. Vaughn had nothing to lose. He already had two murders to answer for. One more wouldn't change his future.

As Vicky held her breath, she realized that these weren't just any voices, they were familiar voices. It sounded like they were on the path just beyond the gardens.

"Ida, all I'm saying is that we don't have to be marathon runners in order for us to be healthy," Rex said stubbornly.

"But we could be," Ida pointed out. "So, why shouldn't we be?"

"Why?" Rex shot back. "Maybe because I miss my knees not feeling like they're going to crumble. Maybe because my poor motorbike is going to get rusty from the amount of time it's spending in the garage. I don't want to spend all of my time straining my body and sweating in the hot sun."

"You don't complain about that when..." Ida began to say.

"Ida," Rex said sharply. "You know that's not the same thing. Look Ida, I think you're amazing. You're stunning. You're perfect, just the way you are. I know you think that you have something to prove, but I don't. I can admit my body doesn't twist and bend like it used to, but it is still just as strong, and that's all that matters to me."

"Now you sound like Vicky," Ida sighed. "Sometimes I think that girl is wise beyond her years."

Vicky felt tears building in her eyes as she heard her aunt speak of her for what she assumed would be the last time.

"She loves you," Rex said firmly. "Like I do. No one is going to judge you if you can't do a triple back flip."

"But I can!" Ida said quickly. "Want to see?"

"Ida, don't, there's something on the

ground..." Rex said. Vicky heard a soft thump. She imagined it was Ida landing on her rear end in the garden. The two were silent for a long moment.

"Are you okay?" Rex asked with concern. "You're not bruised are you?"

"Only my ego," she replied with a short laugh.

"Ida, I don't mind going for a bike ride, or a run, now and then. I'd just like to have time to go for a motorcycle ride, and the energy to enjoy a good stroll through the park. Can you understand that?" he asked.

"I suppose so," Ida sighed. "These are the things you have to deal with, when you're dating an old man."

"Hey, watch it," Rex replied with a playful growl. "I can still chase you, you know."

"I'd like to see you try," Ida teased in return.

Vicky stared into Vaughn's eyes. She could see that he was growing impatient with Ida and Rex lingering in the garden. She hoped that they would stay longer. Suddenly she heard the footsteps stop.

"What's this doing here?" Ida said with concern in her voice.

"I don't know," Rex replied. "But we should get it inside in case it rains."

"I guess so," Ida agreed.

Vicky heard them begin to walk away. Her entire body ached with the desire to cry out, to alert them to her presence, but she knew that if she did Vaughn might kill her, and then turn on Rex and Ida as well. She couldn't put them in danger, no matter how much she hoped that someone would save her. Once their voices faded away she knew her fate was sealed. She looked into Vaughn's eyes, hoping to find some sense of compassion.

"You don't have to do this," she reminded him. "All of this can be over, if you just let me go."

"I'm not going to do that, Vicky," Vaughn said roughly. "I am truly sorry, however. Like I said, this isn't personal."

"Oh, it's very personal," Mitchell said from just behind him. Vicky caught sight of him pointing his gun at the back of Vaughn's head. "Drop the pitchfork," he commanded Vaughn.

"You're making a huge mistake, Detective," Vaughn said darkly. "I will have your badge for this."

"You won't have anything but handcuffs, Vaughn," Mitchell shot back. "Now lower the pitchfork or I will make sure you don't walk out of here alive."

Vicky was staring hard at Vaughn. She was afraid to move as at any second he could drive the pitchfork deep into her body. Being able to hear Mitchell's voice was very comforting to her but she was still scared.

"Fine," Vaughn said and dropped the

pitchfork to the ground. "But you will be paying dearly for this."

"Shut up," Mitchell barked and grabbed Vaughn by the wrists. He quickly snapped handcuffs on him. "I've known you were dirty from the first time I laid eyes on you, Vaughn, and it brings me nothing but pleasure to be the one to take you off the streets."

"The city will suffer for this," Vaughn warned. "I have a lot of friends, a lot of influence. I could change everything."

"You have already changed everything," Mitchell said. "You're a murderer and that's the last thing that our city needs."

Sirens screamed through the air, signaling that Mitchell had called for backup and they were arriving.

"The charges will never stick," Vaughn said. "I'll find a way out of this."

"I promise you, Vaughn, you will not,"

Mitchell said sharply.

"We'll see about that," Vaughn muttered. Mitchell didn't bother to reply. He looked past Vaughn who he held firmly by the cuffs and straight into Vicky's eyes.

"Are you okay?" he asked her softly.

Vicky could only nod. She had never been so frightened. Vaughn had scared her in a different way, because his eyes were so very empty of empathy. Mitchell held her gaze for a long moment, as if to reassure himself. Then he jerked Vaughn away from her and turned him towards the flashing lights. He almost walked right into Sheriff McDonnell who was walking quickly up the path.

"Mitchell, is everything all right?" he asked as he looked from Mitchell, to Vaughn, and then to Vicky who was stumbling along after Mitchell.

"This monster is under arrest for murder," Mitchell said sharply.

"Two murders," Vicky choked out. Mitchell and Sheriff McDonnell looked in her direction with surprise.

"Under the bushes," she mumbled and pointed behind the shed. "It's Margaret."

Sheriff McDonnell grabbed Vaughn hard by the arm and pulled him away from Mitchell.

"You thought you could get away with murder right under my nose?" Sheriff McDonnell demanded. "There's a special place in prison for those who know the law and break it."

"I'll never be behind bars," Vaughn countered sharply.

"I have to tell you, Detective, you've really proven yourself tonight," Sheriff McDonnell said proudly as he ignored Vaughn and looked over at Mitchell. "Not too many cops would risk tangling with a man as powerful as this, but you knew that the law comes first. You did good, Mitchell," he smiled. Vaughn muttered under his breath.

Sheriff McDonnell pulled him towards the waiting police car. Mitchell turned back to Vicky.

"Under the bushes," Vicky whispered again and pointed.

"It's okay," he murmured and pulled her briefly into his arms. "I'm here now. I'll take care of everything," he gestured to Sarah who had come running out of the inn at the sound of the sirens. "Take her somewhere quiet," he instructed her. "She's been through a lot tonight."

"I will," Sarah agreed, her eyes wide. She didn't know exactly what was going on, but she knew it wasn't good. She guided Vicky over to one of the wooden stands in the middle of the garden. She settled her down on one of the benches inside.

"What is it?" Sarah asked in a whisper. "What happened?"

"Vaughn Thomson is being arrested for murder. He killed Roxanne because she walked in on him having an affair with Margaret. Now, he's killed Margaret because Margaret found out the truth about Roxanne's murder. He's a terrible man," she sighed.

"I'm so sorry," Sarah said with a shake of her head. "How did you find out all of this?"

"He threatened to kill me too, Sarah," Vicky said in disbelief.

"I'll kill him myself," Sarah said and started to stand up.

"No, Sarah, it's okay. He's going to see some real justice," Vicky sighed. "I'm sorry about the contest," Vicky said in a distant voice. "Things did not go smoothly."

"Don't worry about that," Sarah said and rubbed Vicky's back soothingly. "Just try to relax. You've been through a terrible experience."

"But Mitchell was there," Vicky smiled faintly. "Even when I didn't think he would be."

"Yes he was," Sarah agreed as she hugged her

sister tightly. "I'm so glad he was."

Chapter Nine

Once the news of Margaret's murder began to spread through the inn, many of the guests began to leave. Vicky and Sarah stayed close to one another in the main lobby. Mitchell was still gathering evidence and questioning witnesses. Vicky was sipping some herbal tea that Chef Henry had whipped up for her. It was soothing, but also reminded her of the conversation that Roxanne had had with Chef Henry. The phone on the front desk began ringing. Sarah picked it up.

"Hello?" she said. "Of course, we'll be waiting for you in the lobby," Sarah said quickly. When she hung up the phone she looked over at Vicky.

"Lauren is on her way down."

"That poor woman," Vicky shook her head. "I don't know how she's going to handle all of this."

Sarah and Vicky watched as Lauren stepped

out of the elevator. She was wheeling a suitcase behind her. She trudged up to the front desk.

"I'm sorry," she said softly. "For all of the trouble."

"You have nothing to be sorry for," Vicky said comfortingly. "You didn't know."

"I should have, though, right?" she looked up at the two women, her eyes red and swollen. "I mean, I am his wife. How could I not know?"

Sarah and Vicky exchanged a short glance before Vicky looked back at Lauren. "Lauren, this man was about to be elected as District Attorney. He had many people snowed. No one knew what he was capable of, and no one would expect you to either. You didn't have anything to do with any of this."

"Thank you," Lauren said shakily. "It's nice to hear that, though I don't know if I believe it. I just think about Roxanne, and our petty competition. Then Margaret, she was sleeping with my husband, but she didn't deserve to die, not like that."

"But you didn't know," Sarah reminded her firmly. "You're not responsible for any of this. It's going to take you time, of course," she added. "But you will begin to heal from this eventually."

"I hope so," Lauren mumbled. "Thank you both for your kindness."

"You're welcome," Sarah said. Vicky reached out and gave the woman's hand a light squeeze.

Outside the inn a horn blared.

"That will be my taxi," Lauren said with a sigh. "Goodbye," she waved to them as she walked out of the inn. Vicky watched her go, and then shook her head.

"Could you imagine being married to someone and knowing so little about them?"

"Marriage can be as terrible as it is wonderful," Sarah pointed out. "It all depends on what you're both willing to put into it. Unless of course you're married to a murderer, in that case it's just all bad."

"I would think so," Vicky nodded. Witnessing the depths of deceit that had existed in Lauren and Vaughn's marriage, Vicky had come to realize that she and Mitchell would never reach that point.

Ida and Rex walked through the side door that led to the pool.

"Vicky, are you okay?" Ida asked as she rushed towards her.

"I'm fine," Vicky promised her and looked at her aunt warmly.

"We were both so worried, but Mitchell insisted we stay back," Ida explained. "I knew, I just knew that you were in trouble."

"What do you mean, Aunt Ida?" Vicky asked.

"I found your cell phone," Ida explained as

she held Vicky's phone out to her. "It was on the path in front of the gardens. I knew that you wouldn't have dropped it. Then I saw what looked like drag marks through the soil. I'm sorry we didn't come for you right away," she frowned.

"I stopped her," Rex explained and rested a hand on her shoulder. "I just thought it would be better if we let the police handle it, because we didn't know exactly what was happening."

"Mitchell showed up before we even had a chance to call him, so he must have been concerned. But he had no idea where you were, we told him that we thought you were behind the shed, and that's when he made us stay put under threat of handcuffs, mind you," she glowered.

"Aunt Ida, he was just trying to keep you safe," Sarah interjected.

"I wouldn't have forgiven myself if anything had happened to you," Vicky explained with a heartfelt smile.

"I think that you know, I would feel the same," Ida sighed. "But the important thing is that you are safe, and that horrible beast of a man is behind bars," she shook her head. "When I heard who it was, I was shocked. Can't trust anyone these days."

"It's not that you can't trust anyone," Rex said gently. "It's that you need to keep the ones you can trust, very close."

Ida smiled up at him and hugged him tightly around the waist. "What do you say we go for a motorcycle ride?" she suggested.

"I'd say I can't wait," Rex replied. "Unless you two need us here?" Rex asked as he looked at Sarah and Vicky. "Is there anything we can help with?"

"Isn't he adorable?" Ida grinned and planted a big kiss on his cheek.

"We're fine," Sarah promised him. "I think the best thing for Vicky is to get some rest."

"No," Vicky said quietly as Ida and Rex walked away.

"No, what?" Sarah asked with surprise.

"No, that's not the best thing for me," Vicky cleared her throat with determination.

"I'm sorry I didn't mean to sound bossy," Sarah frowned. "What is it that will help you to feel better tonight, Vicky?"

"It's not that," Vicky smiled at her sister. "It's that there's only one thing that can make me feel better tonight," Vicky said in a murmur as she looked up at the patio door opening once more. Mitchell strode quickly across the carpeted lobby floor until he reached her side.

"It's official, sweetheart, he's in a jail cell," he said as he took Vicky's hands in his own.

"Oh, I see," Sarah said quietly under her breath and smiled at Vicky.

"I'm so glad it's over," Vicky said and

squeezed Mitchell's hands. "What a weekend."

"Mitchell, why don't you take Vicky to her apartment?" Sarah suggested. "I'm just going to finalize some things here with the paperwork. I'm sure she's pretty worn out."

"Sure," Mitchell nodded and looked into Vicky's eyes. "If that's what you want?" he asked.

"I do," Vicky squeezed his hands lightly. She smiled at her sister as Mitchell guided her towards her apartment. Vicky opened the door and he stepped in behind her. He closed the door. She flipped on a lamp near the couch.

"Are you sure that you're okay, Vicky?" Mitchell asked as he walked closer to her.

"I don't know if okay is the right word," Vicky replied with a sigh. "But I'm better, thanks to you."

"Well, it was Aunt Ida that told me..."

"It was you that rescued me, Mitchell," Vicky

said warmly and patted the couch beside her. He sat down and brushed the hair back from her neck and shoulders. He began rubbing lightly at the tension that had gathered there. "I've been in tight spots before, Mitchell, but I really didn't think I was going to make it out of that one."

"You did," he whispered. "That's all that matters now."

"Maybe, but maybe not," Vicky said calmly.

"What do you mean?" Mitchell asked and sat back slightly.

"I mean, when I was looking into Vaughn's eyes, when I knew he had every intention of killing me, I realized some things about my life," she said quietly and stared off distantly.

"What things?" Mitchell pressed with apprehension in his eyes. "Things about us?" he asked nervously.

"Sort of," she replied and took his hands in hers. Mitchell's face had gone pale, he looked like he was preparing for the worst news of his life.

"I'm always putting off the most important things in my life," she explained as she looked into his eyes. "I'm always thinking that there will be another day, another week, another month, but that isn't always the case, is it?" she shook her head and ran her thumbs along the backs of his hands.

"Not always," Mitchell replied in a murmur.

"So, if I keep putting off the most important things, then I might never have the chance to have them," Vicky said as she studied him. "You're the most important thing in my life, Mitchell. I don't want to wait any longer to get married."

"Really?" he said, his expression lightening. She realized he must have been very concerned about what her intentions were.

"I can't think of a single thing I want more, than to be married to you, Mitchell," Vicky leaned up and kissed him softly. When she broke the kiss he was smiling at her.

"I feel the same way," he said happily. "So, maybe now we can talk about a date?"

"The sooner the better," Vicky said, feeling elated as she wrapped her arms around him. "It's time we had the chance to truly share our lives."

"I can't wait," Mitchell kissed her hard, and Vicky nearly lost her balance from the passion of it. They both laughed as they held onto each other. "It might be a little bumpy," Mitchell warned her. "I can't promise that it will be perfect."

"I don't want perfect," Vicky promised him. "I just want you."

"Aw, that's so sweet," Mitchell grinned, then his smile faded. "Wait a minute, isn't that a little bit of an insult?"

"No," Vicky said innocently. "Like you said, you can't be perfect."

"I said marriage might not be perfect,"

Mitchell argued playfully. "I never said anything about me not being perfect."

"All right fine, you got me," Vicky laughed. "I don't want perfect, I want better than perfect, I want you."

"Much better," he grinned and pulled her in for a long, sensual kiss. After the kiss ended, Vicky rested her head against his shoulder and sighed.

"Oh Mitchell," she murmured.

"Yes Vicky?" he asked, holding her close, his voice filled with heat.

"Don't forget, you promised to help me clean up the shed," Vicky smiled as she looked up into his eyes.

"As long as there are no hammers involved," he grinned in return.

The End

More Cozy Mysteries by Cindy Bell

Dune House Cozy Mystery Series

Seaside Secrets

Boats and Bad Guys

Treasured History

Hidden Hideaways

Heavenly Highland Inn Cozy Mystery Series

Murdering the Roses

Dead in the Daisies

Killing the Carnations

Drowning the Daffodils

Suffocating the Sunflowers

Books, Bullets and Blooms

A Deadly serious Gardening Contest

Wendy the Wedding Planner Cozy Mystery Series

Matrimony, Money and Murder

Chefs, Ceremonies and Crimes

Bekki the Beautician Cozy Mystery Series

Hairspray and Homicide

A Dyed Blonde and a Dead Body

Mascara and Murder

Pageant and Poison

Conditioner and a Corpse

Mistletoe, Makeup and Murder

Hairpin, Hair Dryer and Homicide

Blush, a Bride and a Body

Shampoo and a Stiff

Cosmetics, a Cruise and a Killer

Lipstick, a Long Iron and Lifeless

Camping, Concealer and Criminals

Printed in Great Britain
by Amazon